Barbara Pym died on January 11, 1980. The last few years of her life were spent in an Oxfordshire village, sharing a small cottage with her sister. Between 1950 and 1961 she published six novels, all of which will be reissued in this new series. In 1977, after sixteen years in the wilderness, she published *Quartet in Autumn*. It was treated as a major literary event, as was her next novel, *The Sweet Dove Died*. She had finished revising *A Few Green Leaves* a few months before her death.

Her ordinary people are written about with such detail and kindness that we can gently revel in their idiosyncrasies and admire their quiet but gallant moral standards.
—Jill Neville, *Harpers Queen*

There is a thrill of humanity through all her work.
—Shirley Hazard

. . .the *New York Times Book Review* conducted a survey of what prominent people are reading, and three out of eighteen reported that they were enjoying the novels of Barbara Pym. . . .
—Anatole Broyard

The sparkle they [her novels] had on first acquaintance has been succeded by the deeper brilliance of established art.
—Phillip Larkin

Other books by Barbara Pym

An Academic Question

Civil to Strangers [novella and four stories]

Crampton Hodnet

Excellent Women

A Few Green Leaves

A Glass of Blessings

Jane and Prudence

Less Than Angels

No Fond Return of Love

Quartet in Autumn

Some Tame Gazelle

An Unsuitable Attachment

Very Private Eye: An Autobiography in
Diaries & Letters (edited by Hazel Holt and Hilary Pym)

THE
SWEET
DOVE
DIED

by Barbara Pym

MOYER BELL
Kingston, Rhode Island & London

Published by Moyer Bell

FIRST PRINTING

LIBRARY OF CONGRESS
CATALOGING-IN-PUBLICATION DATA

Pym, Barbara, 1913-1980.
    The sweet dove died / by Barbara Pym.

    p.   cm.
    ISBN 155921-301-9
    1. Triangles (Interpersonal relations)—Fiction.
2. Middle aged women—Fiction. 3. Young men—Fiction.
I. Title.

PR6066.Y58 S9	2002
823'.914—dc21	CIP
	2002035349

Printed in the United States of America.
Distributed in North America by Acorn Alliance, 549
Old North Road, Kingston, RI 02881 (Warehouse-
193 Edwards Drive, Jackson, TN 38301) and in
Europe by Gazelle Book Services Ltd., Falcon
House, Queen Square, Lancaster LA1 1RN England
524-68765

THE
SWEET
DOVE
DIED

To R.

I had a dove, and the sweet dove died;
And I have thought it died of grieving;
O, what could it grieve for? its feet were tied
With a single thread of my own hand's weaving. . .
John Keats

I

'The sale room is no place for a woman,' declared Humphrey Boyce, as he and his nephew James sat having lunch with the attractive stranger they had picked up at a Bond Street sale room half an hour ago.

'Now you're scolding me,' said Leonora, with mock humility. 'I know it was stupid of me, but I suppose it was the excitement of bidding — for the first time in my life — and then getting that dear little book. It was just too overwhelming!'

'And the room was so hot,' James suggested, trying to take his part in the conversation, for after all it was he who had noticed the woman in black sway sideways and almost collapse at her moment of triumph, when she had challenged the auctioneer's rather bored 'Twenty pounds at the table?' with a cry of 'Twenty-five!' Between them James and Humphrey had supported her out of the sale room and after that it seemed the natural thing for the three of them to be having lunch together.

Otherwise it had been a very boring sale, James thought. He had no interest in books and had spent the time idly watching the dealers, hunched over the table in their shabby clothes, making their bids with raised eyebrows or scarcely perceptible movements of hands or catalogues. The other bidders or spectators, mostly men, were crowded in rows on small chairs or standing in corners. A tall man with a slightly raffish air, leaning against the wall, had fixed his gaze on James and was staring at him every time James happened to glance in his direction. James lowered his eyes, feeling foolish but also a little flattered. He was not quite sure if he wanted that kind of admiration and found himself wondering if the diversion of Leonora's near-collapse had saved him from a fate worse than death.

'My dear Miss Eyre,' Humphrey was saying, 'the clerk of the sale would have taken a bid for you, or I'd gladly have done it for you myself if I'd known.'

'How very kind of you—I'll remember that another time. Do you have books in your antique shop?' Leonora asked.

'No. We specialise in porcelain and bronzes and small objects—you know the kind of thing.'

'Objets d'art et de vertu,' she murmured, with a delightful accent.

'Exactly.' Humphrey bent towards her admiringly to refill her glass with the hock he had chosen as being particularly appropriate to the occasion. That this exquisite creature should have been exposed to the contaminating presence of the dealers, for the sake of some trifling little Victorian flower book, hardly bore thinking of and filled him with horror. A *book* sale was certainly no place for a woman; had it been a sale of pictures or porcelain, fetching the sort of inflated prices that made headline news, or an evening sale—perhaps being televised—to which a woman could be escorted

8

after being suitably wined and dined – that might have been another matter altogether.

'And *you* . . .' Leonora turned her gaze upon James. 'You assist your uncle in his business?'

'I'm trying to learn it,' said James.

'Yes, I thought a book sale might be useful experience for him,' said Humphrey. 'One sometimes comes across books at country house sales. What a fortunate accident it was, our coming here today!'

James thought his uncle was making rather a fool of himself. Miss Eyre was certainly of a suitable age for Humphrey to marry, if that was what he wanted, though he had been a widower for so long now that it seemed unlikely he would wish to improve on the convenient arrangements he already had and take such a drastic step as marriage. On this first meeting James admired Leonora very much, particularly the unusual and old-fashioned elegance of her wide-brimmed hat which cast fascinating shadows on a face that was probably beginning to need such flattery. He was attracted to her in the way that a young man may sometimes be to a woman old enough to be his mother.

'You must come and see the shop,' he suggested. 'It's quite near Sloane Square.'

'Indeed, yes, if you happen to find yourself near Sloane Square,' Humphrey joined in, 'and really cne quite often does, don't you think?'

'Certainly,' Leonora said, smiling. 'One does try to arrange one's days so that one visits as many agreeable places as possible and avoids those one dislikes.'

James was surprised to hear her say this and wondered how she managed to 'arrange' her days in this way, when most other people one knew had to work or led dull, housebound lives. Perhaps she had money or was 'kept' in an old-fashioned way like an Edwardian mistress in St John's Wood. Indeed this might well be so, he thought, as he heard her give Humphrey her address.

'Quite a sweet little house,' she said. 'I hope you and your nephew will come and dine with me one evening, so that I can repay your kindness and this delicious lunch.'

They saw her into a taxi — '*straight* home to gloat over my enchanting little book' — and then made as if to return to the antique shop.

'Well, well,' said Humphrey in an avuncular manner, not quite knowing what comment to make to his nephew about a woman to whom they both seemed to be attracted. 'That sale turned out to be more interesting than we expected.'

'Yes.' James laughed in a rather embarrassed way. 'I wonder if we'll ever see her again.'

'Oh, surely.' Humphrey sounded quite confident that they would. 'And now,' he said, hesitating on the edge of the pavement. 'I think I *won't* come back to the shop with you this afternoon. You and Miss Caton can manage perfectly well on your own. It will be good experience for you.'

James said nothing. Everything he didn't particularly want to do was described by Humphrey as 'good experience', but as it was quite likely there would be no customers he supposed he would be able to cope.

Humphrey turned and went away in the opposite direction, smiling to himself. He felt a certain responsibility for James, the only son of his brother who had been killed in the war, and who had quite recently also lost his mother. There was something about the idea of an orphan that brought out the best in Humphrey, that desire to do good without too much personal inconvenience that lurks in most of us. When James came down from Oxford after an undistinguished career and with no particular ambitions, it had not been at all difficult for Humphrey to take him into his antique shop and offer to teach him what he knew. Humphrey's knowledge was not all that great, but it was more than his nephew's complete ignorance. Moreover, James's good looks and pleasing manners were a definite advantage in attracting customers to the shop and persuading difficult American women to buy, and the arrangement was working out very satisfactorily. Humphrey had his flat in Kensington while James lived more modestly in Notting Hill Gate. Their social lives did not impinge on each other to any extent, for an uncle nearing sixty had little in common with a nephew of twenty-four and Humphrey was relieved that he did not have to spend too much of his time with James. Now, for instance, he intended to return to his flat for a short nap, after which he would make his way to his club for dinner and bridge. James, he imagined, would leave the shop at five-thirty, making quite sure that it was locked — though he suspected that Miss Caton, the admirable, fussy middle-aged typist, did not really trust James and would herself be the last to leave — and then either go back to Notting Hill Gate or sample the life of Chelsea, about which Humphrey was vague, for it was some time since he had set foot in the

King's Road, so changed was it now. What James did in his spare time was his own business and Humphrey felt no responsibility there, except to hope that James would have the sense not to get a girl pregnant or be caught smoking cannabis. As he entered his club he dismissed James from his mind, but it did occur to him to wonder how Leonora Eyre spent her evenings. Was she, he asked himself, fond of opera or the theatre? Perhaps that kind of an invitation could be his next move.

James's afternoon followed a boringly predictable course. Nobody came in, the telephone rang once but it was Miss Caton's friend with whom she had a cryptic conversation, apparently about what they were going to have for supper that evening. At half-past five James left, Miss Caton having promised to lock up, and went back to his flat to prepare himself for the evening. He was going to a party given by two old school friends in their Camden Town flat. The door would open, the surge of music and voices would overwhelm him, and he would find himself stuck in a corner with a girl who couldn't hear what he was saying. Not that he could think of anything particularly interesting to say on these occasions, anyway; having been so much with his mother he still found older women easier to talk to. He had certainly not acquired the habit of sleeping with girls and had never smoked cannabis, so Humphrey need not have worried. James was not yet sure what he wanted from life, and had so far tended to avoid violent extremes of any kind.

II

Leonora was also going to a party that night, though of
a different kind from the one James had been invited to.
Hers was just dinner with a woman she had known in
the days when she had a job. The only slightly unusual
thing about it was that Meg's young friend or protégé,
Colin, would be there, as he nearly always was these
days ever since she had taken him under her wing and
befriended him in his many troubles. Tonight a new
friend of Colin's was going to be there as well, which
was perhaps why Leonora had been asked to complete
the strange foursome of two women approaching fifty
and two young men in their twenties.

The name of the friend was Harold and he was of a
bull-like handsomeness, towering over fragile little
Colin with his delicate beauty. Conversation was sticky
at first when Meg was in the kitchen seeing to the meal.
It was obvious that Harold was not of their 'class', but
Colin prattled enough for two, throwing an occasional
private joke to Harold, who sat dumb with shyness and
apparently impervious to Leonora's charm. He seemed
more at ease when Meg came back, her plain good-
natured face flushed from bending over the cooker, and

summoned them to the table. He teased her about the way to a man's heart being through his stomach, and Meg seemed ridiculously pleased. As if the question arose, thought Leonora scornfully. But of course Meg was devoted to Colin and presumably had to put up with his friends as well. There had been quite a number of them over the years – a young man in advertising, a television producer, a civil servant, an Indian, even a curate, once. Leonora could not quite place Harold and wondered what he could be; no doubt she would find out as the evening went on. How different this occasion was from her interesting experience at the book sale and the most agreeable lunch with that charming antique dealer and his nephew! One of these days she would certainly 'find herself' near Sloane Square. But not quite yet. She would wait until exactly the right moment arrived, as it surely would.

'Such a pleasant evening,' she said, at about half-past ten. 'I *have* enjoyed it. I'd no idea it was so late.'

'Now how will you get home?' Meg wondered in the rather vague way that car-drivers do about non-drivers.

'Oh, I shall manage,' said Leonora, with an enigmatic smile as if she had a magic carpet waiting.

Neither of the young men made a move so Meg was obliged to offer to take Leonora herself.

'I can't think how you manage without a car,' she said, perhaps irritated at seeing Leonora standing in the doorway in her dark fur jacket, a square of apricot chiffon draped over her head. Nobody could wear a scarf like Leonora.

Leonora shrugged her shoulders. One simply didn't drive and that was that, but other people were always so kind. And there were taxis. 'I wouldn't dream of letting you take me,' she said. 'I'll find a taxi at the rank.'

'But they always take you the longest way and expect such enormous tips,' Meg complained.

'I've never found that,' said Leonora. 'Taxi drivers are usually *sweet* little men.'

'Well, if you really don't mind . . . ' Meg was obviously reluctant to leave the party. 'I'll just come to the rank with you, to make sure there is one.'

She closed the door of the flat carefully behind her. Leonora said something about the lemon meringue pie which had been so delicious.

'It's Colin's favourite pudding,' said Meg.

Leonora's smile held pity in it. She imagined Meg rolling out the pastry, mixing the filling, beating the egg whites, and all for silly little Colin.

'What did you think of Harold?' Meg asked.

'I didn't really form any opinion. Not Colin's usual type of friend, is he?'

'No.' Meg lowered her voice, though they were out in the street now. 'Most of Colin's lovers' — she brought out the word courageously — 'have been rather different. He's had *such* unhappiness, but I think Harold's going to be very good for him. He works as assistant to a vet.'

'Good heavens!' Leonora exclaimed.

'Yes, really. Didn't you notice his strong kind hands?'

Certainly the hands had been red and solid-looking, Leonora remembered, through being steeped in hot water and disinfectant, perhaps.

'And there *is* a taxi,' said Meg. 'Goodbye, dear. We must lunch sometime.'

Leonora offered her cheek. She did not like being kissed by women, or indeed by anyone very much. It was good to be leaning back in the cool darkness of the taxi. The driver, she now saw, was a coloured man, but she was sure he would turn out to be as 'sweet' as taxi drivers usually were to her.

Meg lived in a somewhat offbeat district, but the tall shabby houses, some of them painted in garish colours, were soon left behind and gave place to discreetly glistening cream or white façades behind one of which Leonora lived. The taxi driver smiled at her large tip and wished her goodnight in a warm soft voice so that she could imagine herself as a beauty of the Deep South being handed from her carriage or as a white settler in the days when native servants were humble and devoted.

She opened her front door and experienced as always the pleasure of being home among the pretty Victorian furniture and objects with which she had surrounded herself. She pitied Meg in her rambling untidy flat with those tiresome young men and wondered whether they had stayed to help her with the washing-up. Colin lived in Paddington, she believed, and presumably Harold lived with him. Meg's flat would seem lonely after they had gone; quite different from her own tranquil solitude.

Leonora liked to think of her life as calm of mind, all passion spent, or, more rarely, as emotion recollected in tranquillity. But had there ever really been passion, or even emotion? One or two tearful scenes in bed — for she had never enjoyed *that* kind of thing — and now it was such a relief that one didn't have to worry anymore.

Her men friends were mostly elderly cultured people, who admired her elegance and asked no more than the pleasure of her company. Men not unlike Humphrey Boyce, indeed.

The wide bed with its neo-Victorian brass headboard was conducive to pleasant thoughts and Leonora arranged herself for sleep. No Bible, no book of devotion, no alarm clock marred the worldly charm of her bedside table. Browning and Matthew Arnold—her favourite poets—took their place with her Guerlain cologne, a bottle of smelling salts, soft aquamarine paper tissues, a phial of brightly coloured pills to relieve stress and strain, and presiding over all these the faded photographs of a handsome man and a sweet-faced woman in late Victorian dress. Leonora had long ago decided that her grandparents were much more distinguished-looking than her father and mother whose photographs had been hidden away in a drawer. Her father had been in the consular service and Leonora's childhood and youth had been spent in various European towns of which she retained many personal memories. Indeed, the recounting of these memories, romantic episodes and encounters, sometimes made her conversation a little tedious, so that people who knew her tended not to mention Lisbon, Dresden or Vienna if they could avoid it. Her parents had left her enough money to live on, so that she did not have to work unless she wanted to. For a time after the war she had taken a job in the same publisher's office as Meg, but seeing school textbooks through the press was an unworthy occupation, Leonora felt. The only thing to be said for work was that it gave one less time to brood and it was supposed to be satisfying for its own sake to the middle-aged. Not that one brooded much. Naturally the thought of death came into one's mind occasionally but one tried to be sensible about it, not getting into a panic, not pushing it away. For a moment Leonora dwelt on the idea of Colin's friend Harold, imagining those strong kind hands putting animals to sleep. Certainly one didn't want to think about *that*. Yet there was no reason why one's death should not, in its own way, be as elegant as one's life, and one would do everything possible to make it so.

III

James was not always as punctual as he might be at the
shop, but for once Humphrey did not comment on it.
He looked pleased and went about humming to himself
and smiling in an irritating way as if he had some secret
business afoot that he wanted to conceal from his
nephew.

At last he could keep it to himself no longer. 'I shall
not be here this afternoon,' he declared, 'but I'm sure
you and Miss Caton will manage perfectly well.'

James thought that they were certainly getting plenty
of practice, but he was not impertinent by nature and
did not say it.

'I am taking Miss Eyre out to lunch,' Humphrey
went on, 'and afterwards to that exhibition at Agnew's
which I think she will enjoy. Rather her kind of
"thing", I should imagine.'

'Yes, I'm sure it will be,' said James mildly. 'Will you
bring her here afterwards? She said she'd like to see the
shop.'

'I might. It depends how things *go*.' Humphrey
looked mysterious, then in case James should misunder-
stand him added hastily: 'She may be too tired to come

down to Sloane Square. I imagine she isn't very strong. She may wish to go home.'

'Oh, quite,' said James, now bored with the subject. 'Do give Miss Eyre my kind regards or whatever seems suitable.'

'I shall certainly do that,' said Humphrey.

Humphrey's invitation to lunch and the exhibition had taken Leonora unawares, before she had been able to 'find herself' near Sloane Square and to pay a surprise visit to the shop. She was a little piqued to have matters taken out of her hands and quite ridiculously disappointed when she found that she and Humphrey were to lunch alone, without James. She had been looking forward to meeting him again – one needed the company of young people sometimes and that of good-looking young men was always particularly agreeable. Being with Humphrey was really not much different from being with any other of her elderly admirers who took her to expensive restaurants and plied her with compliments.

The exhibition was delightful, certainly, family portraits from great houses, and very much to Leonora's taste.

Definitely her cup of tea, thought Humphrey inelegantly, as he watched her admiring the pictures; it had been a good idea.

'Not doing any more bidding, I hope?' he asked in a teasing way.

'Certainly not!' she said. 'I shall get *you* to do all that for me in future. You or James, that is. I hope he's well?'

'James? Well?' Humphrey seemed puzzled, for why should his nephew be anything but well? 'Oh, yes,

James is well, thank you. I left him in charge this afternoon.'

'Could we perhaps surprise him? I'll pretend to be a customer.'

'My dear Leonora' — they had reached the stage of Christian names in the middle of lunch — 'by all means, if you're sure you're not too tired.'

'I might buy a few Christmas presents.'

'Goodness, is it nearly Christmas?' said Humphrey. 'I suppose women start their shopping much earlier than we do.' He thought rather unworthily of one or two things in the shop that Leonora might be persuaded to buy if she were really looking for Christmas presents, but there seemed to be no question of that when they got there. Although she admired a pair of Chinese quails, shuddered at a piece of netsuke, and went into raptures over a Victorian paperweight, she did not ask the price of anything. All that came of it was that Humphrey made a mental note that a paperweight of some kind, perhaps a little less expensive than the one she had admired, might make an acceptable Christmas present for her.

Leonora looked at her watch. 'I ought to be going,' she said. 'One wouldn't want to be caught in the rush hour.'

'I'll run you home,' said James, who had been kept rather in the background up till then.

'Oh, no, my dear boy,' said Humphrey. 'No need for that. My car is parked round the corner.'

'So is mine,' said James, 'and I go in Miss Eyre's direction.'

Leonora stood between the two of them, smiling.

21

People were so kind. 'I mustn't take you out of your way,' she said to Humphrey. 'If James really *is* going vaguely in my direction . . .'

In James's car she leaned back and drew her fur collar up round her neck. He asked if she felt a draught from the open window.

'No, it's just that I like the feeling of fur next to my face.'

'I suppose it must be nice,' said James, who had not experienced it. He felt rather shy, as if her remark had been too intimate for the early stages of an acquaintance, and was unable to think of any more to say.

'Your uncle lives in Kensington, doesn't he?' Leonora asked. 'One wouldn't have wanted to put him to any trouble, especially when he's been so kind.'

'I'm sure he wouldn't have thought it any trouble,' said James. 'After all, it doesn't take long in a car.'

'You live in Notting Hill Gate, I believe?'

'Yes, I've got a flat.'

'You don't live with your family, then? No, of course you wouldn't.'

'Well, I haven't got any family,' said James, embarrassed. 'My parents are both dead.'

'You poor boy.' Leonora was afraid her reply sounded too light and insincere, but what could one say? They drove without speaking for some time until James began to ask her how best to get to her house. When they reached it he got out of the car and went round to open the door for her.

'Would you like to come in and have a drink?' Leonora asked in a cool, almost indifferent tone.

James hesitated. Was she just being polite? he wondered. And did he really want to? He was curious to see the inside of her house and he could pretend a later engagement if it seemed difficult to get away.

'I expect you're going out,' Leonora said.

'No, I'd love to. I only thought it might be a bore for you.'

'My dear James,' she addressed him by his name for the first time, 'would I have asked you if I'd thought that?'

There could be no answer to this so he followed her into the sitting-room. It was prettily furnished with small early Victorian pieces and china and glass objects of the same period. James noticed that the flower book she had bought at the sale was displayed on a little table.

'I open it at a different page every day,' Leonora said. 'It really is so charming. I can't remember now what I chose for today.'

'Pink convolvulus,' said James, looking down at the book.

'And that signifies' — Leonora came to his side and made as if to read, though she knew that she couldn't without her glasses.

'Worth sustained by Tender and Judicious Affection,' James read in a slightly mocking tone, for he was not sure what it meant.

'Let's have a drink,' said Leonora, going to a corner cupboard and bringing out a decanter and glasses.

'You obviously like Victorian things — Victoriana, I suppose I should say.'

'Yes, I adore them. Somehow I feel they're me.'

James looked at Leonora with more interest. She was wearing a soft prune-coloured dress which suited her pale complexion and dark, well-arranged hair. In the more flattering light of the converted oil lamps she seemed younger than in the daylight, or if not exactly young, then of no particular age.

'I think Victoriana do suit you,' he said, 'you look exactly right in that chair.'

Leonora bowed her head in acknowledgement of the tribute, for she was used to receiving compliments gracefully.

'I think *you* belong to some earlier period,' she mused. 'Perhaps the eighteenth century? One can imagine a portrait of you leaning against a ruined pillar.'

'I wouldn't know,' said James, feeling a little foolish now and wishing he hadn't paid her that rather silly compliment.

'You don't look at all like your uncle.'

'No, I take after my mother's side.'

'Golden-brown hair and dark eyes – rather unusual.'

'My mother was American.'

'Really? Do tell me about her.' Leonora expressed what seemed to be a genuine interest, but James was embarrassed at the way the conversation was going. Sympathetic as she was, even he was perceptive enough to realise that Leonora would hardly want to spend the evening talking about his mother.

And now, almost as if she read his thoughts, Leonora gently changed the subject without seeming to and when she suggested that he might be hungry he found himself agreeing that he was.

'I'll see if I can find something for us to eat, then.'

'Oh, but I never expected . . .,' James began. 'And you won't have anything in,' he added tactlessly.

'One always has *something* — tins and packets and eggs, and things in the fridge.'

'I expect people often drop in to see you.'

'Yes, of course.'

'You don't mind living alone, then?'

'No — otherwise I wouldn't.'

James saw that this must be so. There was nothing pathetic about Leonora, and he was as yet too young to assume that a woman living alone is always to be pitied.

'What sort of neighbours have you got?' he asked.

'A young couple on one side and my friend Liz on the other.'

James seemed satisfied. 'So they could get things for you if you were ill?'

'Yes, of course. What happens to you when you're ill?'

'There's a motherly soul in the flat below who likes fussing over me.'

Leonora felt a faint prick of dissatisfaction but made no comment. She had laid the meal — pâté, salad and an omelette — at a round table in the kitchen. James ate heartily.

'I hate modern clinical-looking kitchens,' she said when he remarked how colourful the room was. 'I chose this red paper to make it seem warmer and more lived in.'

After coffee James got up to go. 'I have enjoyed this evening,' he said, and really it was true. There was something remarkably sympathetic about Leonora, even if he was not yet quite sure how to cope with her. 'You must come and see my flat sometime and advise me how to improve it.'

'I should enjoy that,' she said, 'especially advising you.'

They were standing together on the doorstep when a loud harsh cry rent the night air.

'My neighbour Liz breeds Siamese cats,' Leonora explained. 'I should have warned you.'

'How odd – *my* neighbour has a Siamese cat, too.'

'Lovely creatures,' she said, in the tone of one who prefers to admire animals from a distance. Going back into the house she pitied, as she often did, poor Liz whose husband had 'behaved so appallingly' that she now loved cats more than people.

And now there was another sound – men's voices raised in a noisy quarrel. But there was no need for alarm – it was the radio belonging to Miss Foxe who lived on the top floor of the house. It was always too loud but Leonora preferred this violent altercation to the morning religious programme which, with the well-modulated voices singing hymns and the clergyman intoning prayers, always made her feel guilty. Yet it was hardly *her* fault that Miss Foxe should have been already in the house when Leonora came to it and that she was a person of gentle birth and refinement living in reduced circumstances. One just did not want people like Miss Foxe impinging on one's life; no wonder she had not told James about her when he had asked who her neighbours were.

IV

As Christmas approached Leonora found herself wondering whether Humphrey and James, especially perhaps the latter, would do anything to mark the occasion. They might well send a card, possibly a printed one from the antique shop; that was the least they could do, but there were other, more subtle, gradations of behaviour that she might be justified in expecting. At last a card came from James – a Spanish madonna obviously chosen with care, signed just 'James'. Then Humphrey's card arrived – a large Victorian snow scene with his name and private and business addresses printed inside; but 'Humphrey Boyce' had been crossed out and 'Humphrey' scrawled over it in handwriting. Two days before Christmas a registered parcel was delivered containing a paperweight, perhaps the very one she had admired in the shop that afternoon, from Humphrey. It looked charming on her desk downstairs in the sitting-room; but it was James's card that stood on her bedside table.

Christmas Day itself passed in the rather mysterious way that the Christmas Days of middle-aged people without young families usually do pass. Leonora believed that James was spending the holiday skiing in Austria with friends; she did not know what Humphrey was doing nor was she particularly curious. Her own day was spent entertaining her neighbour Liz to an elegant dinner which Liz hardly appreciated, being so much taken up with her cats that she had to leave the table at intervals to see if they were enjoying the turkey liver she had provided for them.

It was a relief to return to normal life again and to get through New Year's Eve, with its feeling of sadness. The days began to lengthen and the first signs of spring appeared. In the meantime social life had started up again, by which Leonora meant her 'new' social life with Humphrey and James. There were visits to sales and exhibitions, theatres, ballet and the opera, and luncheon and dinner parties in Humphrey's flat or Leonora's house. Then Humphrey went abroad on business for a fortnight and when he came back discovered that James and Leonora had been meeting almost every day and had established a curiously intimate relationship. He is like a son to her, Humphrey thought, and since James had lost his mother the situation seemed not inappropriate, though in another way it was as if Leonora, by directing her attention to the young nephew rather than the eligible widower uncle, was showing again that streak of perverseness that had led her to bid for herself at the book sale. One day, Humphrey flattered himself, she would become bored with the novelty of James's youth and realise the more lasting qualities – virtues, almost – of a man nearer her own age who was tall and had kept his figure and was bald only in the most distinguished kind of way.

James saw Leonora as a confidante rather than a mother, somebody to whom he could reveal his hopes and ambitions, such as they were, and most of the happenings of his daily life. Of course he could not tell her quite everything, and she liked to tease him about the parties he went to and the people he must meet — 'your secret life', she called it, as if by making a joke of it she could ensure that he would never deceive her. 'We must find you a nice girlfriend,' she would sometimes say, almost as if she really meant it.

One evening Leonora was sitting alone by the fire reading a novel by Elizabeth Bowen, when the front door bell rang. She knew that it couldn't be James, for he had told her that he was going to a party that evening, which he didn't expect to enjoy. It was comforting to know that if she had hinted that she might be lonely he would have stayed with her, but of course she had urged him to go, saying that she was sure he would enjoy it when he got there, the sort of thing one said to a child. Yet she did not want him to enjoy himself all that much and this thought gave her an almost cosy feeling as she sat with her book, sometimes gazing into the fire. She was annoyed at being interrupted and got up to answer the bell with a bad grace.

Meg was standing on the doorstep. Her manner was extremely agitated. '*Have* you seen Colin anywhere?' she cried, almost in tears. 'I'm trying everyone who knows him, just in the *hope* . . .'

'Why on earth should *I* have seen Colin?' Leonora asked coolly, drawing Meg into the house. 'You'd better come in and get warm and let me give you a drink or something.'

Meg allowed herself to be led to the fire and placed in a chair. Leonora took her old sheepskin jacket, holding it at arm's length as if it were the pelt of a not very clean animal, and hung it up in the hall. Meg looked a sight, she thought dispassionately, in a dusty black polo sweater and baggy green corduroy trousers. Her hair was standing out in a bush and her face was red and swollen and streaked with tears. Leonora averted her gaze as she handed her a glass of whisky – how could she bear to be seen in such a state? 'You look terrible,' she said. 'What's happened?'

A confused story came out. Apparently Colin hadn't been to see her over Christmas, hadn't even come to collect his present, and when she had phoned him he had seemed cold and evasive. That had been weeks ago and she hadn't heard a word since then. There was no answer from his flat and he had ignored two letters she had written.

'I expect he's gone somewhere with his friend,' said Leonora soothingly. 'Harold' she remembered, but she did not specify which friend in case there had been a change.

'Well, he *could* be with Harold and his mother in Gidea Park,' Meg agreed, if a little doubtfully.

Leonora tried not to smile at the idea of Gidea Park, wherever that might be.

'But Harold's mother isn't on the phone, so I don't know what to do.'

'Haven't there been other times like this?' Leonora asked delicately.

'Oh, yes, but never as *long* as this. I'm beginning to think something must have happened to him. Of course

Harold's very jealous, I do know that.'

'I shouldn't worry,' said Leonora. 'You make far too much fuss of Colin, you know.'

'But he's all I've got,' Meg cried, her voice breaking.

Leonora turned away in distaste. Soon Meg would say that she had always longed for a child and in the next instant she did. Leonora regretted having offered whisky; strong coffee, though more trouble to make, would have been just as efficacious.

'Colin's a very selfish young man,' she said, a little smugly, perhaps thinking of James though of course there could really be no comparison. 'He'll be in touch as soon as he needs you again.'

Meg's ravaged face glowed. 'Do you think so?' she said fondly. 'Yes, I expect he will. But it's so awful, this uncertainty . . .'

She seemed about to burst into tears again so Leonora tried to change the subject or at least move to some different aspect of it. 'Why don't you go and have your hair done tomorrow?' she suggested. 'Then you'll be looking elegant when he does turn up again.'

Meg smiled, perhaps at the idea that she could ever be 'elegant', and raised a hand to her head. 'Yes, I must. I know I look awful, but Colin never notices things like that. I've got a bottle of Yugoslav Riesling in the fridge,' she added, 'it's his favourite wine.'

At least he didn't have expensive tastes, Leonora thought. 'Let's have lunch together sometime,' she said. 'I'm sure things will soon be all right. Will you ring me?'

Meg promised that she would and drove away, apparently comforted. Leonora felt she had done some good, an unusual sensation for her and one she rather liked. She settled down again with her book, but her reading mood had passed. It was more agreeable to reflect on how dreadful poor Meg had looked and to pity her unfortunate situation.

James's evening had turned out better than he expected, though it had begun unpromisingly. After arriving at the party and struggling through a solid mass of people, he found himself at a table on which stood some glasses of red wine. Taking one of these and drinking half of it rather too quickly, he looked up to find a girl watching him in a detached way that made him feel uncomfortable. He smiled at her, for it was obvious that neither of them had anybody else to talk to. Her glass was empty and the refilling of it from an anonymous-looking bottle gave him a chance to approach her. The din of the party made conversation difficult and he couldn't be quite sure what her first remark was.

'I'm in the antique trade,' he said desperately, feeling that she had probably asked him what he did but that if she hadn't it was as good an opening as any.

She was rather tall and unsmiling; he gathered that her name was Phoebe and that she had just taken a degree in English at some university whose name he didn't catch. Her shyness disconcerted him though he found her less frightening than the prettier girls who always made him feel ill at ease and inadequate. Those bright mocking eyes, sparkling between the furry layers of false eyelashes, what did they expect of him? Phoebe's eyes were brown and rather dog-like; no doubt they also expected something but it was less obvious what it was.

Phoebe couldn't think why James was talking to her when there were so many more attractive girls in the room; then she realised that they were trapped in a corner and he couldn't escape even if he wanted to. The knowledge depressed her and she gave up trying to talk, turning her face away from him and gazing moodily round the room.

James wondered if he had said something to offend or upset her but couldn't think what. In a curious way he found her attractive and wanted to know more about her. Boldly he suggested that they might leave the party and have dinner together. He remembered reading in one of the Sunday papers about a new Greek 'taverna', and it was here, in a basement decorated with artificial vine leaves and lit by candles, that they sat down in a somewhat unpromising silence. It would have been better, James now realised, to have stayed longer at the party and got a little drunk.

A bottle of wine made things easier and when the food came Phoebe fell on it and began to eat with obvious enjoyment, admitting, rather surprisingly, that she hadn't eaten since morning.

James, who still belonged to the world of regular meals eaten at relatively normal times, wondered why.

'I'm working in the country,' she explained, 'and somehow I didn't get organised.'

James asked what work she was doing and she explained that she had seen an advertisement in *The Times* for a graduate to edit some 'literary remains'.

'Somebody famous?' James asked.

'No—the daughter of a local rich family who died.

She wrote some poems and a journal and her parents are going to pay a publisher to bring out a slender volume.'

'Is it interesting?' James asked.

'Not really. She was in love with some man – you know the kind of thing.'

'Yes, of course,' said James awkwardly. 'Is the village nice?'

'Not bad, but there's such oppressive greenness and too many trees. And all the people are elderly and keep dropping in.'

The idea of the country conjured up an exaggeratedly romantic picture to James; he imagined remoteness and distance until Phoebe explained that the village was within easy reach of London by train or Green Line bus.

James nearly said that he would come and see her but his natural prudence held him back. He could see that he might not want to go into the country in winter, yet he found Phoebe interesting and suggested that they might meet at some future unspecified date. He gave her the telephone number of the antique shop but not of his flat. One never knew. For the same reason he did not kiss her goodnight though he offered to take her wherever she was staying. But she dismissed his offer brusquely, saying that she was spending the night with a friend in West Hampstead, and walking off into the darkness leaving James feeling that he had in some way behaved unchivalrously. All the same he felt that he had made an impression on the girl and he looked on the encounter as something of his own, a private thing that neither Leonora nor his uncle need ever know about.

V

Humphrey and Leonora had been lunching together and now, as it was a fine afternoon, he proposed a drive into the country.

'I shall enjoy it all the more because I shall feel slightly guilty leaving poor Miss Caton to cope with any possible customers,' he declared, 'but who could work on such an afternoon?'

'What about James?' Leonora asked. 'Won't he be working?'

'Not exactly – I've sent him off to have a look round some country antique shops. It'll be good practice for him to see other dealers' stuff.'

'I suppose he'll be incognito,' said Leonora fondly, 'or even heavily disguised.'

'Oh, there'll be no need for that – nobody in the trade knows him yet,' said Humphrey. He hoped they weren't going to talk about James all the time. Indeed, he had chosen this afternoon because he wanted to get Leonora to himself – it was much more suitable that she should spend her time with him rather than with James. As they waited at the traffic lights he leaned over towards her and was about to lay a hand on her when

35

they changed to green and he was forced to attend to his driving.

'Where are we going?' asked Leonora, moving just the merest fraction of an inch away from him. 'Somewhere interesting and remote?'

'Not remote,' Humphrey admitted. 'Interesting, yes, in a way – somewhere you said you'd never been.'

'That might be almost anywhere,' Leonora teased. 'Surbiton or Slough or those places where commuters live.'

'Well, I suppose people could commute from where we're going and probably do. But I shan't tell you till we get there.'

Leonora leaned back in pleasurable expectation. Humphrey's car was very comfortable and the good lunch had made her a little drowsy, but of course it would never do to go to sleep. One simply mustn't allow oneself to drop off . . .

Suddenly – had she perhaps nodded for just a second? – the car turned off and they were among trees.

Humphrey stole a glance at her to see her reaction. At intervals during lunch his lips had curved into a secret smile as he imagined Leonora's pleasure at Virginia Water, her exclamations over trees, water and ruins.

'How beautiful!' She clasped her hands together in a gesture of delight. 'And so quiet and peaceful.'

'Yes, of course one couldn't possibly come here at the weekend – it would be intolerably crowded and vulgar. But in the middle of the week on a working day . . .,' his voice boomed out among the young beech trees.

'A *working* day,' Leonora mocked, thinking how pompous dear old Humphrey was and how much more agreeable it would have been if James had been her companion in this romantic setting. 'A distant glimpse of a temple — perhaps a *ruined* temple — among trees, over still water,' she mused. 'I think that's really one of my favourite sights.'

Dear Leonora, Humphrey thought, so sensitive and impractical. He wondered how many times she had seen such a sight to arrive at the conclusion that it was one of her favourites. Suddenly — he supposed it was the contrast that brought it to his mind — he remembered his dead wife as she had been in her ATS uniform during the war, walking with him among these same trees.

As they strolled along, Leonora keeping up a flow of admiring comments on the scene, they came upon a huge totem pole, shattering the peaceful beauty of the landscape.

What a hideous phallic symbol, Leonora thought, but of course one wouldn't mention it, only hurry by with head averted. There were people clustering round it, too, shouting and exclaiming, a man and two small boys accompanied by Mum and perhaps Gran in white orlon cardigans, with the bright floral prints of their dresses showing through them. How did such people manage to get time off in the week? Leonora wondered.

'I suppose they must be on holiday,' she murmured, as they walked past. She felt a little tired now — perhaps it would be possible to sit down somewhere, but when she mentioned it Humphrey thought the grass would surely be damp — there had been a heavy shower yesterday evening — and suggested they should drive somewhere for tea.

It might not have been so damp in the depths of the

wood, he thought regretfully, imagining himself reclining with Leonora on a bed of pine needles. But he soon dismissed the picture from his mind as impossible and ludicrous. A woodland seduction scene between two middle-aged protagonists could only end in disaster.

'*Tea*,' he said firmly, seeing Leonora's dark beauty against a background of chintz and home-made scones.

Later, when they were sitting in the café he had remembered, he told her that it was here he and Chloe used to meet sometimes.

'Your wife,' she said, her tone reverent to conceal her boredom. She considered it a slight error of taste that he should be able to think of another woman, even one long dead, when he was with her.

'One got a jolly good tea here, even in those days,' he said brightly. 'You know how obsessed one was with food during the war.'

'Ah, the *war*.' Leonora sighed, remembering her 'secret work' somewhere in the south of England before the invasion of Normandy. It had been spring —camellias, azaleas and rhododendrons, and brigadiers making passes at her, and even honourable proposals, among those luxuriant flowering shrubs. Oh, the marriages she could have made, brilliant marriages . . . Of course James would have been only four or five years old at that time, in America with his mother during those early formative years. 'And James was just a baby then,' she said aloud, 'wasn't he?'

'Certainly James was a very young child,' Humphrey confirmed, in an uninterested tone. 'He was with his mother in the United States. His father was killed in the war, you know.'

Of course Leonora had known. 'And then his mother died,' she said softly.

'Yes, but that was later. This date and walnut slice is very good,' said Humphrey, hoping to distract Leonora's attention, 'won't you try a piece?'

Leonora shook her head. The sadness of James's life had taken away her appetite. Really, one couldn't eat with such thoughts. That poor boy, and yet if his mother *hadn't* died . . . 'What a lovely afternoon I'm having,' she said, remembering her duty to Humphrey. After all, James was dining with her this evening; she could afford to be generous.

James approached the village hall cautiously, having first observed from a distance how the land lay. It was of course ridiculous to imagine that one might come upon something of value at a village jumble sale, but one never knew and it was worth trying. It would certainly be more interesting than visiting the country antique shops, 'seeing other dealers' stuff', as Humphrey had put it, for this was the village where Phoebe lived and he intended to call on her. Although they had parted abruptly she had been very careful to write down her address, almost like Eve presenting Adam with the apple.

The first mad rush of the sale was over by the time James entered the hall and paid his admission fee, and as a stranger he felt conspicuous. It was natural that people should stare at him but he wished he had thought of some kind of camouflage so that his head and face need not be quite so nakedly exposed to their curious gazes. Yet if he had worn, say, a panama hat and dark glasses, would he not have been even more conspicuous? Of course the fact of being male singled him out from the crowd of women, most of whom seemed to be shapeless, fat and middle-aged. This did not appear to be the kind of function that men attended, except perhaps the clergy, but no clergyman was visible, only the Scoutmaster with a little group of Scouts and Cubs.

Here, obviously, was where one picked up a Chelsea figure for sixpence, thought James, approaching a trestle table where some bits of china and bric-à-brac were lying. The first object that caught his attention was a salt and pepper set in the form of two cats, with the appropriate holes in their heads, on a little stand.

'That's nice,' said the woman behind the stall, but without much conviction and not at all as if she really expected James to buy it.

'Not quite what I'm looking for,' he said, his eyes straying to other hideous trifles. Would there come a time when even these would be sought after by collectors? he wondered. It might almost be worth buying them up and starting an antique 'supermarket' on his own – rather amusing, but of course his uncle would frown on it.

Evidently there was nothing for him here, but out of politeness he bought a little china castle, though it was chipped, not realising that there was no need to be polite at a jumble sale. He wondered if he should ask the way to Vine Cottage – he was sure any of the helpers at the jumble sale would have been only too pleased to direct him – but decided against it. When after some time he did find it, he sat in his car in the lane before going up to the door.

The tall thin girl in jeans who came in answer to his knock seemed a stranger, only just recognisable as Phoebe, though he remembered the long mouse-coloured hair held back by a ribbon band. But was this the face — pale, peaky and altogether too natural-looking — that had seemed intriguing in the candle-lit restaurant?

She seemed disappointed too, as if he had not come up to her expectations, whatever they might have been.

'So this is the cottage,' he said, looking round the bare little room. It seemed very dark with its small windows.

'The room needs more furniture,' she said. 'I've only brought a few things of my own.'

He wondered which they could possibly be.

'This lamp,' she said nervously.

He glanced at the converted wine bottle as if it were beneath comment. 'You could easily get a few pieces — there are lots of sales round here,' he suggested.

'I might get landed with a case of stuffed birds.'

'And very nice too,' he retorted, slightly on the defensive. 'Victoriana are still quite desirable.'

There was a silence after this rather prim statement. Perhaps feeling that he did not find her as desirable even as a case of stuffed birds, Phoebe began desperately to offer him coffee or a drink but he refused both. 'Would you like to see the garden?' she asked at last.

They strolled out into the overgrown garden. James remarked on the vine which sprawled over the back of the cottage.

'Yes, that's why it's called Vine Cottage, I imagine. Is it all right, do you think, with those woolly grey buds?'

'Of course — don't you know the poem about the red

turning gray?'

'No,' she said brusquely, obviously feeling that she ought to have known.

'It's Browning, but perhaps he isn't thought much of now.' James was about to quote the lines when he remembered that it was one of Leonora's favourite poems – that was how he had come to know it – and some kind of natural delicacy held him back.

'Are you any good at gardening?' she asked.

'No,' he said quickly, seeing himself having to mow the lawn, 'but my mother was a great gardener.'

No doubt his mother was dead, Phoebe thought, giving him an unfair advantage over her, with a mother alive in Putney.

The walk round the garden did not take long and soon they were back in the cottage.

'You haven't seen my bedroom,' said Phoebe, leading the way up the steep, narrow stairs.

Standing in the little room, which had a sloping ceiling and walls patterned with wistaria, James put his arm round her shoulders, thinking that she was just a little too tall for him. He kissed her and after a few murmured endearments things happened so quickly that he could not afterwards have said who had taken the initiative. James had certainly not meant to go so far but she had been so eager. She had really 'thrown herself at him', as somebody of an older generation – Leonora, of course – might have said. At the thought of Leonora a shadow crossed his face. He turned away from Phoebe and contemplated the pile of books on the floor by the bed. How untidy she was! He must get her a little bookcase or a table – he had one himself that would do

42

very nicely.

Phoebe, feeling him turn away from her, raised herself up on one elbow to look through the window.

'What's the matter?' James asked. 'Somebody coming?' He sat up, nervous. For one wild moment he pictured his uncle entering the room. 'Ah, James, my dear boy . . .'

'It's all right, it was the vicar's housekeeper. On her way to get the fish fingers for the evening meal, I shouldn't wonder. Anyway, she's gone past now. What are you looking at?'

'This window's nearly closed up with leaves — couldn't you get somebody to cut them away? It can't be healthy,' he said primly. 'Insects might come in when you're asleep.'

'Oh, I'm hopeless at getting things done,' said Phoebe. 'I suppose now you'll say how untidy the room is.'

'Well, you could do with somewhere to put those books. I could probably let you have something.'

'You?'

'Yes; the lease of my flat is up soon and I'll be putting some of my things in store while I go on a trip abroad for my uncle.'

'What sort of furniture could you lend me?'

'Oh, a bedside table, and a little Victorian chair covered in olive green velvet — you'd like that, I think.'

'Desirable Victoriana — not quite me, but still.'

'Then there's a mirror with cupids, fruitwood — that's rather pretty.' Leonora had always admired it excessively; perhaps it was unwise of him to have mentioned it. 'I ought to be going,' he said.

43

'I suppose you've got a date this evening.'

'Yes, I have, in a way.' Dining with Leonora didn't exactly count as a 'date'.

'I could make you a cup of tea.'

'That would be nice, but hadn't you better . . .?' He looked at her bare shoulders doubtfully. 'Somebody might call.'

'They might, too. This village believes in dropping in. I suppose this sheet would do as a sarong but I don't seem able to arrange it properly.' Phoebe struggled back into her jeans and put on a crumpled white cotton shirt. 'Is that better?' He must still have looked doubtful for she said rather crossly, 'Oh, well, it'll do to make tea in,' and crept barefoot down the stairs.

James waited uneasily in the sitting-room. He began to feel that he had behaved most unwisely. Why had he let himself get entangled with Phoebe like this? Yet what was 'entangled'? Surely he need not feel any obligation towards a girl who had thrown herself at him?

'Will you come again?' she asked frankly. 'Or perhaps you'll invite me to your flat sometime?'

'Yes, I'll do that – we could have dinner. I'll give you a ring.'

'Then I can see the furniture!' She laughed. 'How practical I'm being. Shall I come out to the car with you?'

'Not with your bare feet.'

'All right, I'll just kiss you goodbye here. Oh James, what did we do?'

What indeed? he wondered, as he drove back to London. He hoped there wouldn't be any traffic jams,

44

for Leonora would expect him to be punctual. She hated him to be late. That was the worst of being attached to an older woman, though 'worst' was surely the wrong word to use in connection with anyone as delightful as Leonora.

VI

There was a little park near Leonora's house and it was here that she had asked James to meet her, so that they could have a walk before dinner. He had agreed rather unwillingly and now he felt decidedly tired after his exertions in the country and would have preferred to sink into a chair with a drink at his elbow rather than traipse round the depressing park with its formal flowerbeds and evil-faced little statue — a sort of debased Peter Pan — at one end and the dusty grass and trees at the other. Wasn't it a slight affectation on Leonora's part to find it so 'agreeable' and the statue so 'appealing'?

'*There* you are, darling — and just a little late. Did the traffic hold you up or something? One knows how it can at this time of day.'

James bent his head to kiss her. A faint breath of heliotrope — Leonora's favourite *L'Heure bleu* — came to meet him. He wondered if she noticed anything different in his manner; a hint of Phoebe's scent lingering about him might arouse her suspicions. Then he realised that Phoebe didn't use scent and he had changed and had a bath; his imaginings were old-fashioned and ridiculous like a novel of the thirties.

'Well, there was traffic, of course,' he began, feeling guilty and trying to remember what he had done after leaving Phoebe. He had gone straight home and prepared himself to meet Leonora, he thought, his sense of virtue tinged with cynicism. There hadn't even been time for a drink. 'You look wonderful in that colour,' he said, moving away from her to admire the amethyst-coloured dress she was wearing. 'It's autumnal, somehow.'

'You mean that I look old? That I'm in the autumn of life?'

'You know I didn't mean that! And anyway autumn is a much pleasanter season than spring or summer, much more *agreeable*.' He smiled as he used one of her favourite words.

Leonora looked up at him affectionately. 'Did you enjoy going round the country antique shops today?' she asked.

'Yes, quite. I suppose I might have bought something, but I just priced the things, and then I found myself driving through a village where there was a jumble sale going on, so I went in there.' James stopped, afraid that he might go too far.

'And did you find some rare treasure?'

'Only a little china castle and that was cracked.' A bit like Phoebe, perhaps. What was Leonora like? A piece of Meissen without flaw? It would be an amusing game to liken one's friends and acquaintances to antiques.

'Humphrey won't be very thrilled with *that*,' said Leonora. 'I'm sure you're not supposed to go to *jumble* sales, my love.'

'I know – I got drawn into this one, somehow. But

you can bet that if Humphrey had gone he'd have found something special. He always has better luck than I do,' said James disconsolately.

'You can hardly say that—after all, you both found *me*, didn't you?'

'Yes, of course, at Sotheby's that day. How was your expedition with Humphrey this afternoon?'

'Lovely! We went to Virginia Water. All those trees and distant ruins, so much *me*.'

'I wish we were walking in some beautiful garden now,' James sighed.

'Some *giardino* or *jardin*—perhaps the Estufa Fria in Lisbon.' Leonora smiled. 'That funny old Professor —did I ever tell you?'

Leonora had had romantic experiences in practically all the famous gardens of Europe, beginning with the Grosser Garten in Dresden where, as a schoolgirl before the war, she had been picked up by a White Russian prince. And yet nothing had come of all these pickings-up; she had remained unmarried, one could almost say untouched. It was all a very far cry from the dusty little park where she and James now walked.

'And then there was Isola Bella—that tree with the great leaves—*Elefantenohren* . . .' She broke into laughter at some memory James could not share.

He glanced up at the undistinguished trees around them. 'Haven't we had enough of a walk now? It's getting dark—somebody's blowing a whistle and it looks as if that man is about to lock the gates. We don't want to be locked in, do we.'

'Don't worry, he's a sweet little man and he's often opened the gate for me. There's no need to hurry.'

48

Nevertheless James felt that the man was not very pleased at having to unlock the gate for them. Obviously it was only with Leonora that he was 'sweet'.

'How charming your house looks,' said James, as they approached it.

'Yes, doesn't it — and do you know, I think I'm going to be able to buy it soon, so it will *really* be mine and I can do what I like with it.'

'Will you have to buy Miss Foxe with it?'

'Yes, but one hopes to be able to get rid of *her* pretty soon.'

Leonora spoke so forcibly that James gave her a startled look.

'Here she is,' she whispered harshly, as they entered the front door.

James saw a white-haired, fragile-looking woman of about seventy, wearing a grey dress and a string of perhaps good pearls, who appeared to be struggling to lift a paraffin can up the stairs.

James ran forward. 'Do let me carry that for you,' he said.

'Oh, how kind! It really is heavier than I thought.' She had a fluty, well-bred voice.

'Much too heavy for you to carry,' said James gallantly. 'She shouldn't have to do that,' he said afterwards to Leonora.

'Darling, you're so thoughtful and one loves you for it,' said Leonora in her coolest tone, 'but *what* a fuss. It was only a two-gallon can and it couldn't have been so very heavy. And anyway what on earth does she want with paraffin at this time of year?'

'Well, I suppose it's cheaper than electricity or gas and

49

the evenings are still rather chilly,' he said.

'Oh, very chilly,' Leonora mocked. 'One feels that using paraffin at all is somehow degrading – the sort of thing black people do, upsetting oil heaters and setting the place on fire. Really, it's rather frightening to think of her up there – that's why one will simply have to get rid of her when her lease runs out.'

James made a faint murmur of protest. One day Leonora would be old herself, but obviously it wouldn't be the same.

'One has to be tough with old people,' Leonora went on, 'it's the only way – otherwise they *encroach*.'

'Don't let's talk about her,' said James uncomfortably. 'I feel I've earned a drink.'

A few minutes later he sat relaxed with a gin and tonic, enjoying Leonora's conversation flung at him from the kitchen where she was putting the finishing touches to the meal. They had a cosy arrangement of telling each other of the day's happenings, either by meeting or by telephone, but James could not be as frank as usual about his day and was content to listen to Leonora describing in detail her expedition with Humphrey to Virginia Water. He really did not want to say much more about the village jumble sale and hoped that one or two amusing observations would be enough and that he could be left to enjoy his drink and gaze around him at Leonora's pretty room.

It was a pleasing setting for her, with its pale green walls and trailing plants – for naturally Leonora was 'good' with house plants. Some of the pieces of furniture had come from Humphrey, but James himself had provided a few trivia or 'love tokens', as she called them, and he supposed that was what they were even though it was she who had labelled them thus. Her love of small Victorian objects made it easy for James to find suitable trifles to express his devotion.

'Asparagus!' he exclaimed, as she came out of the kitchen with a dish. 'The first this year.'

'Then you must have a wish.'

James was embarrassed, as one usually is when commanded to make a wish.

'A *secret* wish of course, darling,' Leonora reassured him.

I have no secrets from you, was what he wanted to say but the glib words would not come. Whatever would a meal with Phoebe be like? he wondered, when Leonora brought in the next course which was chicken with tarragon.

'You're looking particularly handsome tonight,' she teased. 'I wonder how many people have fallen in love with you today?'

One at least, he thought uncomfortably. To his chagrin he felt himself blushing, and yet by now he was quite accustomed to this particular kind of teasing from Leonora. Sometimes it seemed almost as if she had created him herself—the beautiful young man with whom people were always falling in love and who yet remained inexplicably and deeply devoted to her, a woman so much older than he was. James had been content to play this part and of course there was no doubt of his devotion to Leonora. But now there was Phoebe—or was there? It was certainly not part of Leonora's plans for him, if she had any, that he should become devoted to a younger woman. But somehow the word 'devotion' didn't seem applicable to what had taken place in Phoebe's cottage this afternoon.

James was relieved when Leonora came back from the kitchen with a chocolate mousse, a favourite dish she often made for him. No need to brood over Phoebe now. Afterwards there would be coffee and perhaps music or just talking. Sometimes James would tell her about his childhood in America or read poetry to her while she toyed with a piece of tapestry work, her beautiful dark blue eyes looking up at him over the tops of her glasses. The glasses had become a joke between them — 'one's failing sight, so middle-aged'.

Tonight James had with him a copy of Sotheby's catalogue, describing a forthcoming sale of furniture which he thought would interest her. Reading from sale catalogues was another of their favourite diversions and there was nothing Leonora liked better than to hear James's pleasing voice reading out the seductive descriptions which brought the beautiful pieces before her eyes — narrow crossbandings of tulipwood, palm tree motifs and eagles cresting . . . the poetry of the phrases flowed over her in a delightful confusion so that she hardly knew what was being described, only that it was something exquisitely desirable, and that this was being another of their 'lovely evenings'.

VII

Leonora had little use for the 'cosiness' of women friends, but regarded them rather as a foil for herself, particularly if, as usually happened, they were less attractive and elegant than she was. When Meg rang her to arrange a meeting for lunch, her first instinct was to make an excuse, but since she had become friendly with James she had felt increasingly curious about Meg's relationship with Colin. Then, too, she had not seen her since the evening when Meg had called on her in such distress. Presumably Colin had now 'come back', or however one would express it, and certainly Meg sounded happy, almost exuberant, when she asked Leonora to meet her at a snack bar in Knightsbridge at a quarter to one.

Leonora was her usual few minutes late, though not as late as she would have been if meeting a man. Meg was one of those women who are always too early and can be seen waiting outside Swan and Edgar's, with anxious peering faces ready to break into smiles when the person awaited turns up.

'*There* you are!' she exclaimed, as Leonora strolled to meet her.

Leonora greeted her but did not apologise. Meg was looking tidier than when they had last met. She was wearing a light spring coat in a shade of green that did not suit her particularly well, but her hair had been newly done and – or so it seemed to Leonora – the grey streaks disguised with a brown rinse.

'You'll never guess why I suggested we should meet *here*,' said Meg.

'Well, it's convenient for Harrods and one often wants to go there.'

Meg looked blank. Obviously Harrods meant nothing to her. 'It's Colin,' she explained. 'He's got a job here.'

Leonora expressed surprise; perhaps congratulation also was called for, but she would keep that in reserve until she knew more of the circumstances.

'We must go downstairs,' said Meg, 'where they have the salads. Do you mind? You take a tray and choose what you want from the counter.'

Leonora followed her into a dimly lit basement whose orange and purple walls were hung with abstract paintings. Behind the counter she was just able to discern two figures – a long-haired girl wearing round tinted glasses – however did she manage to see anything? – and Colin. Both were serving out raw salads from a number of dishes.

'Hullo, Leonora,' said Colin smoothly. 'What are you going to have?'

'I don't know – what *is* there? Some pâté, perhaps, and what do you think would go best with it? You must help me choose.' Leonora was at her most appealing, but in the dim light it was hardly possible to see what the

54

dishes contained. Colin was also at his most appealing and Meg beamed proudly at the sight of him, so efficient and charming in a pink flowered shirt.

'A friend of Harold's got him the job,' she explained, when they had settled themselves at a cramped little table in a corner. 'He seems to be doing very well and he *likes* it, which is *so* important.'

'Hardly the kind of thing to make a career of, though,' said Leonora, looking around her. This was most definitely *not* her kind of place, she decided — everyone so young, the girls appallingly badly dressed by her standards, all talking too loudly in order to make themselves heard above the background of pop music. 'Surely you don't come here often?' she asked.

'Well, it's a bit far from the office,' Meg admitted, 'so I don't come *every* day. But when Colin first took this job I think it gave him confidence to know that I was here. And of course it's so *good* for one, all this' — she indicated the coarsely shredded cabbage on her plate.

Leonora felt she would have said the same had it been grass they were eating. 'I gather then that things are better,' she said delicately.

'Oh, *much* better. Just a sort of misunderstanding really, that's all it was. You have to let people be free,' said Meg, in the brave manner in which she had spoken of Colin's 'lovers'. 'In that way they come closer to you.'

Leonora smiled but said nothing.

'We went out to the theatre last night,' Meg went on. 'Colin and I and Harold and his mother.'

'That must have been a strange party.'

'I suppose it was, when you come to think of it. And

the show wasn't *really* what I'd have chosen myself,' she named a musical which had been running for over a year, 'but it was an interesting experience.'

'Does one really want to have "interesting experiences" at our age?' Leonora asked. 'I'm not sure that *I* do.'

'Oh, you're different. You must have had so many already, living abroad and always being so much admired,' said Meg generously.

Leonora smiled again, more warmly this time, though she was less pleased when Meg went on to say that she didn't think of Leonora as the sort of person who had 'experiences' now.

'How do you think of me, then?' Leonora asked.

'Just living in your perfect house, leading a gracious and elegant life,' said Meg. 'It's hard to explain,' she added, seeing a shadow of displeasure cross Leonora's face.

'You make me sound hardly human, like a kind of fossil,' Leonora protested.

'I didn't mean that — it's just that I never think of you as being ruffled or upset by anything. Not like me — that awful night when I burst in on you, whatever must you have thought!'

'People react in different ways. One may not *show* emotion, but that doesn't necessarily mean that one doesn't *feel* it.'

'I'll get us some coffee.'

While Meg was away Leonora thought over what she had said. She was not sure that she liked the picture of herself it suggested. Of course one wasn't like that at all, cold and fossilised. It was only that all one's relationships had to be perfect of their kind. One would never have put up with anything as unsatisfactory as Colin's behaviour, for instance.

'*Not* the best coffee in London,' said Meg apologetically, returning with two cups. 'I thought it safer to get it black. Look how busy they are now — Colin says it's murder between one and two.'

'What a good thing we came early, then. This has certainly been an "interesting experience" for me.' Leonora touched her immaculately tidy hair and drew on her gloves.

'*So* glad you've enjoyed it. We must do it again some-time.'

They parted outside the snack bar — Meg to return to her office, Leonora to wander round Harrods. She was tempted, being so near, to pay James a surprise visit at the antique shop, but she restrained herself and was rewarded when she returned home by a telephone call from him, arranging a meeting for lunch next day in 'their' little restaurant near the shop.

That evening Leonora was having supper with her neighbour Liz. It seemed that her whole day had been spent with women less fortunate than herself, she thought, as she sat in Liz's back room listening to the cats crying and wailing in their pen in the garden.

They would settle themselves down for one of Liz's long drinking sessions before there was any hope of anything to eat, Leonora knew from experience. The cats would be in and out of the room and Leonora would try to avoid getting one on her lap, kneading at her skirt with its claws. Liz's own clothes were of course so much plucked by cats that the pulled threads gave an almost bouclé effect to everything she wore. Eventually Liz would embark again on the subject of her unhappy marriage. 'All that love, *wasted*,' she would say. This was one of the rare occasions when Leonora would feel inadequate, having no experience of her own to match it. She had never been badly treated or rejected by a man—perhaps she had never loved another person with enough intensity for such a thing to be possible— whatever the reason she would keep silent, only observing that perhaps love was never wasted, or so it was said. Liz for her part would be equally bored by Leonora and her reminiscences of her Continental girlhood and later attachments mysteriously hinted at which never seemed to have come to anything. Yet at the end of the evening each woman would feel a kind of satisfaction, as if more than just drink and food had been offered and accepted.

VIII

James hardly knew whether his visit to Phoebe had been a success or not. Their awkward love-making in the cottage bedroom seemed very far removed from the world of Humphrey and Leonora, and while he was not particularly anxious to repeat the experience he liked to think that he could if he wanted to. It gave him confidence to feel that he had a girl hidden away in the country that nobody knew about. Humphrey even made it easier for him by sending him round to country sales, which he himself found boring, to see if there was anything worth buying.

One afternoon he had called for Phoebe to take her to a sale and they were going into a house to view the contents.

'It seems so awful,' she said, 'all these people tramping through the hall with their muddy feet.'

James looked at her in surprise. It was the sort of remark Leonora might have made, with her fastidiousness and feeling for atmosphere. He had always imagined from the untidiness, almost squalor, of her cottage that Phoebe was incapable of noticing muddy footmarks on tiled floors. It gave him an uneasy feeling, as if the two women in his life were merging together in some curious way.

He explained to Phoebe that the house had belonged to an old lady, now dead, so that there could be nothing personal about it.

'All the same, a relative might be lurking,' she said. 'You never know.'

James led her off to look at some china — there were good pieces of Coalport and Worcester and something that might have been Dresden, but she preferred a crude pair of Staffordshire dogs.

James was examining a figurine when a man and woman came up and greeted him.

'Hallo, James, what are you after?' asked the man.

'Oh, my uncle thought there might be something,' James mumbled.

'But you're not letting on what it is,' said the woman, in a light brittle voice.

'Those flowered bedroom sets might be worth going for,' said the man, indicating a ewer, basin and chamber pot patterned with purple irises.

James looked round furtively. Phoebe was some distance away, as if she had removed herself purposely. Perhaps it would not be necessary to introduce her. James hoped not, for she was — as so often — looking somewhat unworthy of him in a very short cotton dress and sandals. The couple — Richard and Joan Murray — were friends of Leonora's and sold Victoriana at their shop in the King's Road, hence, perhaps, Richard's affectation of interest in the bedroom china. James was glad to learn that they had only dropped in to have a look and did not intend staying for the sale.

Phoebe had been pretending to examine some bundles of old books as she watched James talking. Jealousy flared up in her as she realised how little she knew of his world.

'Anything you like there?' said James awkwardly, as he came back to her.

'I always feel I'd like to collect old books,' said Phoebe, 'but then when I look inside them I'm repelled.'

James wondered if perhaps there was a little flower book he could get for Leonora but there was no time to examine them for the sale was starting. The auctioneer mounted the rostrum and with evident enjoyment began to play his role.

The larger things, garden effects and most of the furniture, had already been sold in the morning and now the more interesting smaller lots came up, glass and china, books and other oddments. James began bidding for a Coalport basket of flowers but there were two dealers against him and he became discouraged. Eventually a set of plates was knocked down to him but the comparative lack of opposition made him nervous of his uncle's comments in case there should be something 'not quite right' about them.

'Shall we go now?' he whispered to Phoebe. 'We can find somewhere to have tea.'

In the village a Trust House stood back from the wide main street, but for some obscure reason James did not suggest going into it. And yet the reason was not so obscure, for it seemed the kind of place where the Murrays might have stopped and he did not wish to risk another encounter. Fortunately Phoebe did not suggest it either and it was not until they had reached the next small town that she exclaimed, 'This might do — if you can park here.'

'You mean the Leopard Dining Rooms?' asked James doubtfully.

'Yes, it looks the kind of place where you might get a strong cup of tea to restore you after all that bidding.'

'All right, then — there doesn't seem to be anywhere else.'

'Oh, this is fabulous,' said Phoebe with uncharacteristic enthusiasm. 'Shall we sit in the window?'

There were a few other people in the café, some looking rather uneasy, as if regretting that they had not entered the Trust House.

At least it looked fairly clean, James thought. Was this Phoebe's setting — plastic tablecloths, artificial flowers and bottles of sauce? he wondered, for she seemed happy and relaxed. Certainly it could never be Leonora's.

When the tea came it was of a strength and darkness that reminded one more of meat extract than of some delicate infusion of leaves from India or Ceylon. James sipped his cautiously as if afraid that it might poison him.

'I suppose we could have had fish and chips, like those people at the table in the corner,' Phoebe whispered, passing him the plate of thick bread and butter.

'Would you have liked that?' he asked, not quite sure if she was joking.

'No, of course not. Won't you try one of these op art cakes?'

James declined and felt as if he were being prim and

fussy, seeing her apparent enjoyment. He felt almost resentful towards her, for while in a way she was 'sending him up' she also seemed to be dragging him down by her easy acceptance of the place. In a way he was enjoying it too but it was the sort of thing that only seemed to be fun at the time. Afterwards he would be ashamed of having had tea with her in the Leopard Dining Rooms.

'Are you happy?' she asked with disconcerting suddenness when they were driving back to the cottage.

'What a question!' he said, hoping that she would interpret his answer in the way that pleased her most.

'I'll go and get out the drinks,' she said, running ahead of him.

'You've got some new cushions,' said James, following her into the room. They were bright and garish, not at all the sort of thing anyone one knew would choose, yet Phoebe looked almost exotic reclining among them, like a vamp in an old film with her heavily made-up eyes and inviting expression. Making love to her was like an amusing unreal game, so far removed from his everyday life that he could not feel his usual guilt.

When after some time Phoebe sat up and said with a rather distressing lack of purpose, 'I suppose we ought to have something to eat,' the image of Leonora returned, and even more of the delicious 'little something', always ready or made in a moment, that she invariably produced whenever one called on her.

James noticed a cold joint standing on the table by the open window, very much exposed to wandering animals, and he had seen a cat prowling around outside. There was also a bowl of lettuce from which he

63

surreptitiously removed a few inedible-looking leaves which seemed to have earth adhering to them. Phoebe was obviously not at her best in the kitchen. It was a mistake to assume that all women were. The kitchen itself was not very clean either. There was the washing-up from lunch or breakfast or both, two unrinsed milk bottles, eggshells not thrown away, paw marks on the sink and cats' hairs floating in the atmosphere. James began to feel that he was not so hungry after all.

All the same, he managed to eat what was provided — Phoebe's rough red wine helped it down — and afterwards lay happily with her among the bright cushions. He wondered whether he should stay the night, then he remembered the encounter with the Murrays at the sale and a feeling of uneasiness came over him. Waking up next morning in the Bohemian discomfort of the cottage would certainly not be agreeable, he decided.

Going back into the room after he had gone, Phoebe made ineffectual attempts to tidy it and even to clean up the kitchen, for she had sensed his disapproval, but in the end she became bored. One of the village cats had come into the room and jumped up on top of the big old-fashioned radio set which Phoebe turned on, making music for herself and warmth for the animal. A symphony was being played and as Phoebe lay watching the cat she had the fancy that its spreading body was like a great empty wineskin or bladder being filled with Mendelssohn. She began to think of a poem she would write for James.

It was a pity he couldn't tell Leonora about the cat filled

with music, James felt, as he smiled over the poem Phoebe had sent him. That was the only bit he really understood and it might have been appropriate for this afternoon when he had promised to take Leonora to a cat show, where Liz was exhibiting some Siamese kittens. Although he didn't particularly want to go – there were many pleasanter ways of spending an afternoon, he felt – it seemed a good opportunity to appease his conscience for the lie he had told Leonora about having come straight back from the sale and spent the evening with one of his useful old school friends.

'Just kittens and neuter cats,' said Leonora, reading from the programme, 'that sounds so cosy, doesn't it?'

'Shall I be the only grown-up male thing there, then?' James asked, not altogether joking.

'Probably, darling – though one doesn't think of you as male, exactly. Not all tweedy and pipe-smoking and doing carpentry at weekends.'

'No . . .' James could appreciate the accuracy of her distinction but there were other, more attractive, aspects of maleness, he felt, that Leonora might have mentioned.

The hall where the show was being held was hot, crowded and noisy. James looked around him with dismay at the prospect of having to spend the afternoon there. It is a truth now universally acknowledged that owners grow to look like their pets, and it was certainly impressed upon him as he and Leonora pushed their way through the crowds surrounding the cages in their search for Liz and her brood of Siamese.

'*There* you are, Liz darling!' Leonora proffered her cheek to the little dark woman who stood before them with a tray of cat litter in her hands. 'I've brought James, as you see.'

She might have put it the other way round, James felt, seeing that *he* had brought *her* in his car. He was conscious of Liz's critical eyes on him and wondered, as always, what she was thinking. He always felt a little uneasy in her presence, perhaps because, as a divorced woman, she was known to have a great contempt and dislike for men. But if, as he remembered, he was not to be thought of as male he need have no fear.

'Lovely to see you, James,' she said, 'and what do you think of my babies?'

Two litters of kittens, making ten in all, were sleeping in the cage, twined and curled up into a great clot of cream and brown, with a blue eye studding it here and there like a jewel.

'Very pretty,' said James. 'Have the judges been round yet?'

'They're on their way.' Liz indicated two stout women in white coats followed by a girl acolyte bearing a yellow plastic bowl of milky-looking disinfectant. 'I'm pretty confident of this lot. Wouldn't you like to buy one?'

'Yes, James, you ought to have a cat,' Leonora urged.

'I don't think I could cope,' said James weakly, imagining the malevolent creature ruling his life that the kitten might become. 'Besides, I'm going away soon.'

'James is going on a tour of Spain and Portugal,' Leonora explained, as if he were a child. 'Humphrey thought it would be a good thing for him to have a look at the Continental stuff.'

'Oh, that reminds me,' said Liz, 'Joan Murray's here. You know how she *dotes* on cats. She got Dickie to bring her but he didn't stay.'

Rather sensible of Dickie, James felt, wondering if he should mention having met the Murrays at the country sale. It might be easier to say something before Joan did.

'Leonora! How heavenly to see you—and *James* too!' Joan Murray was upon them before he could get out his carefully casual sentence. 'Don't tell me Humphrey's here? No—men must work, obviously —Dickie just dropped me here and fled.'

James looked down at the ground, feeling even less manly than before.

'Wasn't it funny seeing James at that sale?' said Joan.

'You didn't tell me,' said Leonora, with a hint of reproach in her tone.

'No, I must have forgotten,' said James lamely.

'Well, that *is* flattering,' Joan protested. 'I obviously made *no* impression.'

James joined uncertainly in the general laughter. Had she seen him with Phoebe? he wondered. As far as he could remember Phoebe had been some distance away when Joan and Richard had come up to him. To his relief Joan now left the subject. Apparently there had been another sale with much more amusing things.

'Dickie found the most marvellous old flowered *loo*,' she prattled. 'So we're going to put it in the window and fill it with bulrushes and pampas grass.'

Leonora promised to visit their shop, though, as she admitted afterwards, she thought Joan and Dickie rather tiresome and silly. 'You never told me you'd met them,' she repeated to James, as they were walking round the show, and now perhaps there was more than a hint of reproach in her tone, what with the heat and noise and her feet hurting a little.

'I'm afraid Joan was right – it just didn't make that much impression,' said James rather crossly.

They had stopped in front of a cage where a cat-like shape shrouded in a cloth lay fast asleep. How much wiser to contract out altogether, James felt, as this creature had evidently done. Or to sit stolidly in one's earth tray, unmoved by the comments of passers-by. Yet too often, like some of the more exotic breeds, one prowled uneasily round one's cage uttering loud plaintive cries.

Leonora looked up at James anxiously and saw that he was frowning. This characteristic sign of displeasure made her realise that she had gone too far. It had been a mistake to repeat her complaint; obviously James couldn't be expected to tell her every detail of his life and secretly she was pleased that meeting Joan had made so little impression on him. 'Do you think Liz would mind if we slipped away?' she said.

'No – let's do that. I'll give you tea at my place.'

'I should like that. And we might go through your things.'

'Are you sure you can cope with all this?' James asked as they were having tea. 'Mrs Jelly did offer, you know, and she's on the spot.'

But, darling, she doesn't *know* your things like I do — besides she's much too busy.' Leonora smiled as she remembered how she used to feel almost jealous of the woman who lived in the flat below James, until she had met the excellent Mrs Jelly, cosy, motherly, but thoroughly unattractive and much occupied with her job as corset buyer for one of the big stores.

'Well, of course I'd much rather you did it, if you really feel you can,' said James. 'I'll take my personal stuff or leave it with Humphrey.'

Leonora's glance strayed to the photograph of his mother and rested there awhile. No doubt he would be taking *that*. It always disturbed her to think that this young woman, with the curly hairstyle and dark lipstick of the early fifties, so well remembered by Leonora herself, should be James's mother. They had talked about her in the early days of their acquaintance, when James had told her of their closeness and of her sudden tragic illness and death, but now she was taken for granted and aroused no more interest than the rather bored reverence accorded to Humphrey's dead wife Chloe in her ATS uniform. All the same, how fresh and young she looked now when Leonora was feeling the effects of an exhausting afternoon.

'I'm rather tired, darling,' she said. 'Please, James, would you take me home?'

'But of course,' he said, 'we'll go now.' Trailing round that cat show had been too much for her, obviously, and he could see that she was tired. He noticed for the first time some new lines on her beautiful neck, and he took her arm rather gently, as if she were some old fragile object that needed careful handling.

IX

One morning some days later James arrived at the shop to find his uncle and Miss Caton in a state of considerable agitation. It appeared that the premises had been broken into during the night and a number of things stolen.

Humphrey was wringing his hands as he sat on a Hepplewhite chair in the room at the back of the shop, recounting the losses in a tone of lamentation.

'Those quails,' he moaned, 'ah, those quails!'

'You don't mean . . .'

'Yes, my dear boy, I *do* mean . . . those *quails.*'

They had been Chinese and rather valuable, James remembered. He was a bit vague about their provenance and altogether rather nervous about the Chinese things, not knowing much about them and not really liking them, though he had never dared confess this to his uncle.

'I've just made a cup of tea,' said Miss Caton, who was crouching near the gas-ring. 'This will do you good – a strong cup of tea with plenty of sugar. I learnt that when I was doing first aid during the war – treatment for shock.'

Humphrey glanced distastefully at the tan-coloured liquid in the thick white cup and waved it aside. 'No, thank you, Miss Caton — I really couldn't drink it — and where *did* you get that *terrible* cup?'

'It's the one I have my elevenses and my tea out of every day,' she said briskly.

Humphrey took his mid-morning coffee elsewhere if he was not at a sale and was seldom on the premises in the afternoon either, so he had probably never noticed his typist drinking from the thick serviceable cup.

'Well, Miss Caton,' he said, 'I can only hope that nobody has ever seen you drinking from such a monstrosity. It would hardly be a good advertisement, would it?'

'I take my tea in the back,' she said, on the defensive, 'so no customer could have seen me.'

'And you, James — do you drink from such a cup?' asked his uncle sternly.

'I don't know,' James mumbled. 'I suppose I may have done on occasion.'

Humphrey exclaimed in horror.

'Perhaps a cup of *China* tea,' Miss Caton persisted, 'though it wouldn't have the same reviving effect, and without milk or sugar it might well be too acid for you in your present condition.'

James felt they were wasting time, though he was not sure what they ought to be doing. He felt ineffectual and guilty at having arrived after the others, as if he could have prevented the theft by having come ten minutes earlier. Now Miss Caton pressed the rejected cup of strong tea on him and he found himself drinking it almost as a punishment. It was not at all nice and by now not even hot. The tea at the Leopard Dining Rooms had been better than this.

'What about the police?' he suggested.

'Oh, I've done all that,' said Miss Caton. 'I discovered the theft, you see, when I arrived. At quarter past eight,' she added a little smugly. 'The CID came immediately in response to my 999 call. Two most charming men, in plain clothes, of course. They told me I'd done *quite* right not to touch anything. It's so horrid to think of those burglars touching our lovely things with their nasty rough hands.'

'It's quite likely that the thieves were men of taste,' said Humphrey, 'or at least of some knowledge. They took the very best netsuke, you know. That *ram* . . .' He moaned again. 'So they would probably not have had rough hands.'

'Perhaps Miss Caton didn't mean it literally,' James suggested.

'Well, no, perhaps not in the literal sense of labouring men who work with their hands. In any case they would have been wearing gloves—such delicate objects as those quails would require most careful handling.'

There was a call from the shop. 'Anyone here?'

'Good heavens, is the door open?' said Humphrey. 'Go and see who it is, James, while I get on with this inventory. Miss Caton, will you take dictation on to the typewriter, please.'

James hurried guiltily into the shop, for it was he who had forgotten to lock the door when he arrived. A florist's delivery boy was standing gaping at a bronze of two naked human figures in a complicated embrace. A sheaf of white roses and carnations tied with mauve ribbon had been put down on an inlaid rosewood table. James picked them up hastily. 'Are these for us?' he asked. 'Are you sure you've got the right address?'

'That's what it says,' said the boy, now on his way out.

James saw that the flowers were indeed addressed to his uncle. Remembering to lock the door this time, he went back with them.

'How exquisite!' said Humphrey, taking a card from the little envelope attached to the sheaf. 'And isn't that just like dear Leonora – who but she would have thought of sending flowers at a time like this? She must have done it immediately after I telephoned her with the dreadful news.'

'What has she put on the card?' James asked.

' "With kind thoughts and deepest sympathy in your sad losses," ' Humphrey read out. 'So *right*, somehow.'

James wanted to smile at the words but did not like to. 'Unusual to send flowers,' he remarked. Who but Leonora, indeed.

'I'll arrange them in that blue and white vase,' said Miss Caton.

'Ah, yes, the Worcester,' said Humphrey.

'Shall you be going to Sotheby's this morning?' she asked.

'Oh, no – it's only "Valuable Printed Books",' he picked out the words scornfully, 'today. There's far too much to be seen to here.'

Nevertheless Humphrey left for an early lunch and declared that he would not be back until late in the afternoon. He was gratified to see that there was a small paragraph in the early editions of the evening paper about the robbery. The reporter had quoted his own words about the thieves evidently being men of taste.

'Don't you think a lot of people may come in this afternoon?' James asked, realising that he was to be left on his own.

'One hopes that people won't come out of vulgar curiosity,' said Humphrey, 'but if any do the prices are clearly marked. It must be business as usual,' he added, as he left the shop.

Which would mean that he would have to sit in the front, on view to passers-by, James realised, for if he did not sit in the shop he would have to be in the back with Miss Caton and hear about her friend who was receiving instruction in the Roman Catholic faith, which was her latest topic of conversation. ('And she said to the priest, "But supposing it's Friday and I've got some liver to finish up?" That floored him, I can tell you!') Even with the relaxation of the fasting rules Miss Caton would still have too much to say, so James chose to sit in the shop.

It was a rather hot afternoon, the sort of time when work of any kind seems disagreeable. James was tired from the events of the morning and from the effort of sorting things out in his flat to be put into storage or lent to Phoebe and Leonora. He was inclined to be sleepy and even nodded into a doze once or twice. Two American ladies passed the window and he could hear them speculating as to the prices in dollars. As four o'clock approached he wondered if he could slip out to the pâtisserie round the corner for a cup of coffee rather than endure Miss Caton's tea, but decided he had better not. After a while he went to the window and removed a little tortoiseshell and silver box he had earmarked for Leonora's birthday. He took it back to the desk where he had been sitting and began to examine it more closely. Seen in this way it appeared to be not quite perfect, as he had at first thought; there was a slight flaw where a bit of the silver inlay had come away. It was really more the kind of thing Phoebe might appreciate. Leonora liked things to be flawless, expected them to be. He began to wonder if so exquisite a person was really capable of packing up the things in his flat and dealing with the removal men. It seemed too much to ask of her and yet he must not forget that she had offered to do it — he had not even had to hint at it. She would take one or two things for herself and the rest would go to the furniture depository. Then Phoebe could go and choose what she wanted, apart from the things he had already suggested for her.

The hot afternoon dragged on. Then a man entered the shop quickly, almost stealthily, and asked the price of a paperweight in the window. James recognised him as the man who had watched him at the sale where he and Humphrey had first met Leonora, and on various other occasions. This was the first time they had met at close quarters. He told the man the price of the object and they made some perfunctory conversation. Then the man made a suggestion which brought a not unbecoming blush to James's cheek, though it was not the first time such a proposition had been put to him. If his suitor had been more attractive, and if Miss Caton had not come in at that moment, who knows what might have happened. As it was the man mumbled something about a friend being interested in the paperweight and left the shop as quickly as he had entered it.

'Oh, that man — he's always hanging round here,' said Miss Caton, with an impatient gesture as if she were brushing away an insect. 'You don't want to have anything to do with people like that.'

Even though he was inclined to agree with her James resented her nannyish attitude and the tea in the thick white cup which she now brought him. He drank it hurriedly, now particularly conscious of its unsuitability in such surroundings.

Suddenly, as if the day had not already held more than enough, he saw Phoebe standing looking into the window, obviously nerving herself to come in.

His first feeling was one of panic. A man sitting in a shop, perhaps especially in an antique shop, is in a vulnerable position. It had not occurred to James that Phoebe would ever come to London uninvited. He had always thought of her in the country, in the dark little cottage rooms, or sitting under the vine in the back garden, not here, near Sloane Square, where Leonora might appear at any moment. For an instant he imagined the horror of their meeting — Leonora, cool, poised and exquisitely dressed, Phoebe, shy, on the defensive and in her odd clothes, and he unhappily in between. What would they say to each other? Obviously it must never happen. As Phoebe opened the door and came in he remembered with relief that Leonora was dining out this evening with an old admirer, one of those respectable pick-ups in the great gardens of Europe, so she would be safely out of the way. He could take Phoebe to his flat and out to dinner and then put her on to a train at Waterloo.

Humphrey did not encourage 'followers', so James's

greeting of Phoebe was a little constrained. He did not kiss her, but took her hand and murmured something vaguely affectionate.

'What are you doing here?' he asked.

'Oh, I couldn't bear the country and Anthea Wedge's journal any longer, so I decided to come and see you, then go and stay the night with Mother.'

In Putney, he remembered she had once told him and he had thought it was perhaps not where one would care to have one's mother live.

Phoebe looked even more skinny and droopy than usual in a rather unbecoming beige crêpe dress which was in the fashion of that summer but yet reminded him dimly of his mother at some unspecified period of his early life. The dress was obviously new and he noticed that she had put silver varnish on her nails. Her appearance was touching and upsetting and he found himself longing to make love to her.

It was five o'clock — time to leave the shop, but too early for dinner. He decided to take her to his flat for a drink.

His sitting-room was depressingly untidy with piles of books and objects on the floor. When they were inside they kissed awkwardly, as if for the first time.

'I like your dress,' he said, 'very fashionable.'

She glanced at him suspiciously. 'But the colour doesn't suit me.'

'No?' Of course it didn't, or she needed different make-up or something. Leonora always knew what suited her, almost boringly so. James would have liked to advise a woman what to wear but didn't know where to start with Phoebe.

She wandered round the room, seeming ill at ease.

'This is nice,' she said, picking up a gilded wooden figure from a Spanish church. 'Can I borrow this?'

'My uncle will probably want to have it in the shop,' he lied, knowing that Leonora wanted to keep it for him.

'Oh. Couldn't I choose the things I'd like to have now?'

'Well, it's a bit complicated. You won't mind going to get them out of the furniture depository, will you? You'll rather enjoy it, I should think,' he added, imagining her in those gaunt surroundings.

'How do you expect me to *enjoy* anything when you won't be here?'

'Oh, Phoebe, I'm not going to be away all that long,' said James, wishing she wouldn't be so intense.

'Is that woman who lives below going to pack up your things?'

James did not answer.

'It's so sad to think of your flat being empty and you far away,' she persisted.

'The flat would have been empty anyway because the lease runs out,' said James sensibly, 'and I want to find another when I get back.'

'Where will you go till you do?'

'To my uncle's — he has plenty of room.'

'You won't have to live over the shop?' she asked, suddenly in a joking mood. 'Or with Miss Caton?'

'No, I won't.'

Phoebe had taken up the photograph of James's mother and was examining it. 'I can't believe this is really your mother — she looks so young.'

'Well, she was – comparatively.'

'That black lipstick and matching nail varnish and those rows of pearls – it all looks remoter now than the Victorian age. Poor girl, she never lived to see you grown up.'

'I think it's time we went and had something to eat,' said James, fearing, not for the first time, the power of Phoebe's imagination. 'Where shall we go?'

'Oh, anywhere – you decide.'

The restaurant James chose was one of the many Italian trattorie, small and crowded with tables rather too close together, and decorated with strings of Chianti bottles. The young waiters darted about, responding with charming politeness to the halting holiday Italian some of the diners felt obliged to practise on them. The hot summer evening was made even hotter by the flames heating up various dishes which also gave a spurious air of distinction to the restaurant, as if exotic concoctions were being created at the tables when it was often no more than a portion of frozen peas being warmed up.

James picked up the menu. 'What do you feel like?' he asked.

'Nothing, really,' she said unhelpfully.

'That isn't much good,' he said, running his eye down the list of Italian specialities.

'I meant that it was enough just to be with you.'

'Thank you,' he said gracefully, wishing that he had thought of saying it.

'I can't expect you to share the feeling,' she burst out in her frank way. 'All I really want is a glass of water and a roll – it's that sort of day.'

James, looking back over his day, decided that the end of it at least could be improved and that he deserved rather more than that. Afterwards they went for a walk, strolling hand-in-hand down Kensington Church Street, looking in the windows of the antique shops. In one he pointed out to her a pair of vases he admired and would like to possess.

'Perhaps I could give them to you,' she said.

'They cost rather a lot of money,' he said, laughing. 'I went in and asked.'

'I suppose somebody could afford to give them to you,' she said. 'Your uncle, perhaps?'

'No doubt — but he doesn't value me quite as highly as that. And now I suppose I'd better take you home.'

'I love your old-fashioned manners,' she said, mocking. 'You surely don't mean to come all the way to East Putney?'

'But of course,' said James, a little daunted, but hailing a taxi none the less. It might have been better to have gone back for his car, but a close embrace in a taxi would make it easier to tell her that this would be their last meeting before he went away. But of course it was not easier and they finished the long ride still with nothing said. At least he had given her a good dinner.

'I'll ring you,' he said, uttering that useful goodnight formula.

He had made the taxi wait, intending to allow himself the luxury of taking it all the way home, and he stayed only long enough to give her a last quick kiss on the doorstep before the door of the quiet suburban house opened and a grey-haired woman, who looked as if she had been waiting for this moment, drew Phoebe inside.

Frowning a little, as if at something vaguely un-satisfactory, James settled down for the ride back, watching the figures tick up on the clock.

In bed Leonora held the telephone receiver in her hand and heard James's number go on ringing. Obviously he was out. She had been obliged to put off her dinner engagement because she had felt she was getting one of her headaches, a sort of migraine she occasionally suffered from. Probably the heat and the prospect of a not very interesting evening had brought it on. Now she longed for James to come and see her, to sit quietly by her bed, perhaps laying a cool hand on her forehead or reading aloud to her in his beautiful voice.

She put the receiver down, disappointed and a little annoyed. Now that James was going away she felt the need to spend as much time with him as possible. She thought he would have wanted it also, then she remembered that she had had an engagement for this evening and he was not to know that she had put it off. Perhaps he had gone to the cinema, which she disliked anyway, so that was 'all right'. She lay back again and was nearly asleep when the telephone rang. She snatched up the receiver, but it was only Meg. Evidently she was alone too, Leonora thought, not realising that for an instant she was making an absurd comparison between herself and James and Meg and Colin.

Meg just wanted an excuse to go on about Colin and what hard work it was for him at the snack bar. She really thought he would have to give it up if things went on like this. Now they were short staffed in the kitchen and he had to cut up raw vegetables — 'you should just see his hands, all stained and brown, it's really too bad'—and how was Leonora? she enquired belatedly.

Leonora did not feel inclined to go into that and brought the conversation to an end. She was awake now and Miss Foxe's radio, playing something unsuitable, made sleep impossible. What a relief it would be when her lease ran out and she could get rid of her! The thought of it did much to relieve Leonora's headache and she found herself sufficiently recovered to sit up and re-do her nail varnish. But those brown spots on her own hands — unlike the stains on Colin's — were surely a sign of age? The headache began to return and she lay down again, the tears trickling slowly down her cheeks.

X

James left for his tour of Spain and Portugal full of advice and letters of introduction from his uncle and warnings from Leonora as to what he should or should not eat and drink. Once in the plane he not unnaturally experienced a sensation of freedom, almost of escape, at the thought of being on his own for several weeks. Nevertheless, such was his nature, the first thing he did on arriving in Spain was to send postcards to Leonora and Phoebe, telling the former that he had arrived safely and that everything was wonderful but that he missed her, and the latter that everything was wonderful and that he had written to the furniture depository, telling them that she would be coming to choose the pieces he had promised to lend her for the cottage. He did not say that he missed Phoebe, feeling that she would not expect it.

To be involved with a man's furniture, especially to have some of it in one's possession, even if only temporarily, adds considerably to one's prestige, which was perhaps why Phoebe had asked her friend Jennifer to go with her to the depository which was situated in north-west London, somewhere beyond Cricklewood.

Phoebe had talked a great deal about James and the antique shop and what beautiful things he had in his flat, so that Jennifer expected something rather special to be revealed when a tea chest was opened for them and Phoebe began to delve inside. It seemed to contain a great many newspaper-wrapped bundles. The first one she chose to investigate was an awkward but promising shape, as if it might be a figurine or small statue, or even a carefully padded piece of glass.

'Oh . . .' The unwrapped newspaper disclosed some old cork table mats, a bottle opener with a comic head and a number of spoons and forks with the plating worn off. 'Perhaps this.' Phoebe took out another, larger bundle. It turned out to be a lamp made from a Portuguese wine bottle. 'He always despised mine so,' she said in a puzzled tone, 'and yet it looks as if he had one himself. I don't remember noticing it.'

'I expect he hid it away somewhere. It wouldn't go with all those beautiful antiques.'

'Yes, I suppose that was it. I wonder what *this* is?'

It proved to be another wine bottle lamp, this time a straw-covered flask.

Jennifer tried not to smile. James's wonderful 'things' were not living up to expectations, so that she now began to doubt other aspects of the affair that Phoebe had told her about.

'This tray,' Phoebe went on, 'art nouveau, isn't it?' That at least was respectable. 'And here's a little glass bird.'

Italian tourist stuff, thought Jennifer; she had brought one back herself from a holiday in Venice.

'I wonder where his other things are,' said Phoebe,

unwrapping three undistinguished ashtrays. 'I remember seeing all kinds of objects that don't seem to be here.'

'Perhaps his mother has them,' said Jennifer, in a rather bitter tone.

'But his mother's dead – he's an orphan.'

'Poor James.'

'He was very devoted to his mother.'

'He *would* be! Perhaps some other relation, then – his uncle or a *friend*.'

There was an uneasy silence.

'That doesn't seem very likely,' said Phoebe uncertainly, for how did she know?

A man now approached from the far end of the gallery carrying some small articles of furniture.

Phoebe's face brightened. 'Oh, look, here's the little table and the Victorian chair – but where's the fruit-wood mirror with the cupids? I thought I was going to have that.'

'I think Miss Eyre took it, Miss,' said the man stolidly.

'*Jane* Eyre?' asked Jennifer. 'I don't like the sound of *that*.'

'Miss Leonora Eyre,' said the man. 'Unusual isn't it, that name, Leah-Norah.'

'Those Leonora overtures,' went on Jennifer gaily. 'I never did like Beethoven. The mixture of that and Jane Eyre is rather *disquieting*, don't you think?'

'Oh, don't be silly. It's probably the woman who lives in the flat below James – an old thing about sixty. I once met her on the stairs. She was always fussing over him and I suppose he thought she might like to have something. All the same, I should hardly have thought that fruitwood mirror was her style. I wish I could remember her name though,' she added a little uneasily. 'I don't think I ever knew it.'

'Well, we can't do anything about it now,' said Jennifer impatiently. 'I expect you'll find out sooner or later.'

Phoebe arranged with the man for the furniture to be sent to her at the cottage and then the two girls went off to have tea with Jennifer's mother at a teashop in Wigmore Street. Jennifer speculated on the idea of Jane Eyre supervising the packing of Mr Rochester's furniture and from there went on to imagine other heroines in similar situations. Phoebe listened perfunctorily, for she was preoccupied with the idea of Leonora Eyre and wondered how she could find out for certain who she was.

XI

The fruitwood mirror was, of course, very much Leonora's style. The glass had some slight flaw in it, and if she placed it in a certain light she saw looking back at her the face of a woman from another century, fascinating and ageless. It might be a good idea to use it when she made up her face, to spare herself some of the painful discoveries she had lately been making – those lines where none had been before, and that softening and gradual disintegration of the flesh which was so distressing on a spring or summer morning.

Today she had to·go to the dentist, Mr Lambe, an old friend who admired her even under the difficult circumstances of their twice yearly encounters. He was a spare, handsome man who collected netsuke – perhaps there was something tooth-like about the little discoloured ivory carvings which could explain their attraction for him. He spoke enthusiastically of his latest acquisition as he stuffed Leonora's mouth with cotton wool and inserted the draining tube before filling a tooth.

'A wooden wasp in a rotten pear!' he chanted. 'Now wouldn't that description attract any collector! Unfortunately I was unable to get to the sale – now how does that feel? Just clench your teeth together, please, Miss Eyre – is that quite smooth? And would you believe it, it went for two-fifty! *Two-fifty!* Luckily I was able to acquire it off the dealer who'd bought it. Wasn't that a *tragedy*, the burglary at the gallery! *Poor* Mr Boyce!'

Mr Lambe also attended to Humphrey's teeth and had lately been visited by him, so he had heard all about the loss of the quails. Leonora closed her eyes as he began to drill for another small filling. Two fillings at one visit – even her beautiful teeth were going now. 'Those quails,' she heard Mr Lambe droning, 'such exquisite objects. The thieves must have been men of considerable discernment. Such a robbery is in a different category altogether from the petty thefts one hears about in the suburbs.' Mr Lambe came from one of these himself, though he did not see himself as doing so.

'I suppose a thief of discernment might steal netsuke even in the suburbs,' Leonora remarked, 'though a petty thief wouldn't know their value.'

'No, a small-minded person wouldn't necessarily be attracted to small objects,' said Mr Lambe. 'He'd be more likely to steal a television set or a canteen of cutlery.'

Leonora closed her eyes again. It was a hot afternoon and the discomfort of the fillings combined with Mr Lambe's conversation had made her feel rather faint. When the receptionist appeared with her scarf and gloves, Leonora could sense the girl watching her critically as she arranged the scarf carefully around her neck.

'You look rather pale, Miss Eyre,' said Mr Lambe. 'I

88

should go and have a cup of tea. There are several delightful places in Wigmore Street.'

Of course Leonora knew several such places where elegant women like herself and a few idle elderly gentlemen could pass an hour drinking coffee or tea and eating cakes. How fortunate that Mr Lambe had not forbidden eating and that she would be able to have one of her favourite cakes, delicate worms of chestnut purée and cream on the lightest of foundations. It was surely for times like these that such delights had been concocted, for she was hardly in her usual spirits after an exhausting time at the dentist and no James to cherish her. While waiting for her tea to be brought she took out the postcard he had sent her, so affectionate and tender and missing her, writing soon and of course *all* his love.

'This is the place,' said Jennifer, 'and there's Mother. She looks as if she's been waiting *ages*.'

'I'm sorry we're late,' said Phoebe, looking around her suspiciously. This was not at all her kind of place, but she brightened up when the waitress approached their table with a tray of cakes, her tongs hovering.

Leonora from her corner looked annoyed, for she had been there longer and should have been served first. Still, she had her tea and that was a comfort.

'I'm going to have one of those marron things,' said Jennifer. 'Oh, but there seems to be only one – would you like it, Phoebe?'

'No, you have it. I'd rather have a strawberry tart.'

The waitress went over to Leonora's table. 'I'm sorry, madam,' she said in answer to her request, 'that young lady over there had the last marron gâteau.'

'Oh, but this is really too annoying,' said Leonora petulantly. 'I've just been to the dentist — I can't eat anything hard.'

'None of the gâteaus is *hard*, madam,' said the waitress reproachfully. 'They're all fresh today.'

'Well, then, a coffee éclair.' Leonora glared — and even a person as lovely and gracious as Leonora could do this when the occasion demanded it — in the direction of the table where Phoebe and Jennifer and her mother were sitting. But the undistinguished-looking women, the older one inelegantly surrounded by shopping, the younger ones dressed most unsuitably for town and carrying flower-patterned paper carrier bags, seemed hardly worthy of her attention and she soon forgot them in the pleasure of the éclair, which was almost as delicious as the marron confection would have been.

Only a retired Brazilian diplomat, the type of man who could spare the time for afternoon tea, sitting at a table midway between the protagonists, noticed the little drama, if such it was. Now what have I seen? he asked himself. Something or nothing? A beautiful woman disappointed over a cake, a mere triviality, really, and yet who could tell . . .?

Leonora finished her tea and took a taxi home. As she approached her house she noticed with irritation Miss Foxe's dingy 'Jacobean' chintz curtains blowing out of an upper window. How wonderful it would be when the house was all her own! As she prepared a light supper, Leonora found herself imagining what she would do with those extra rooms. Then the telephone rang. It was Humphrey, asking if he might come round and see her as he was afraid she might be lonely.

How kind people were, Leonora thought, setting out a tray of drinks and preparing to receive her visitor. Coffee and brandy, perhaps? She herself preferred crème de menthe; she had changed into a green chiffon dress which gave her a feeling for that drink.

Humphrey had brought a china plate for her — something he had picked up in Portobello last week — just a trifle, but he thought it might amuse her. Leonora was delighted with the Victorian scene of ladies under a tree; a cedar tree, they decided.

'Oh, to have lived in those days,' she lamented.

'My dear Leonora, you'd have found it *most* disagreeable,' said Humphrey firmly. 'You have this romantic view of the past — and of the present, too,' he added.

'Yes, I suppose one feels that life is only tolerable if one takes a romantic view of it,' Leonora agreed. 'And yet it's wicked, really, when there's all this misery and that sort of thing, but one feels so helpless — I mean, what can one *do*? As it is, one tries to lead a good life. . . .' She paused, dissatisfied with the phrase, for somehow it conjured up a picture of Miss Foxe going out to church early on a Sunday morning and that had not been at all what she meant. 'One enjoys the arts and gives something to charity, of course, and' — here she bowed her head over her crème de menthe — 'one loves people to the best of one's ability . . .'

Humphrey let her refill his glass in the pause that followed. He did not quite know how to say what was in his mind. 'You mean, you love James,' he said, which was *not* how he had meant to put it.

'Yes, of course one adores darling James,' she said, with more than her usual affectation.

'But it's so unreal, my dear, this loving James. Surely you must know that nothing can come of it?'

'One would hardly expect anything to "come of it", as you put it.'

'It's such an unnatural relationship,' Humphrey went on, 'an attractive woman of your age and James . . .' He was uncertain what to say about his nephew whose sexual inclinations had never been quite clear to him. 'So much younger than you are' — that at least was true — 'and one day he'll want to get married to a girl of his own age, no doubt, and then where will you be?'

'One doesn't look so far ahead,' said Leonora faintly, 'but of course I should be the last person to stand in James's way if he ever wanted . . .'

'But *I* want,' said Humphrey suddenly. 'You know that.' He moved nearer, his bulk looming over her.

He is going to kiss me, Leonora thought in sudden panic, pray heaven no more than that. She tried to protest, even to scream, but no sound came. Humphrey was larger and stronger than she was and his kiss very different from the reverent touch on lips, cheek or brow which was all James seemed to want. One couldn't lose one's dignity, of course, Leonora told herself, for after all one wasn't exactly a young girl. Surely freedom from this sort of thing was among the compensations of advancing age and the sad decay of one's beauty; one really ought not to be having to fend people off any more. But this was of little comfort in the present situation, and now Humphrey's hand, that hand so accustomed to appraising objects of art and of vertu, had strayed inside the neck of her dress and would certainly have torn the delicate chiffon, if nothing worse, had not a gentle knocking on the door caused its hasty withdrawal.

Miss Foxe's way of tapping, so very genteel and apologetic, had often irritated Leonora in the past. And even now, though her main feelings were of relief and gratitude for the interruption—almost Divine intervention—she could not entirely control her usual annoyance at Miss Foxe's stupidity. For surely she must have known that Leonora had somebody with her when Humphrey's car was so obviously standing outside the house and the hall filled with the smell of his cigar.

Humphrey had sprung up from the sofa and was standing looking out of the window when Leonora opened her door, so that Miss Foxe did not see him immediately. When she did, her apologies were profuse—of course she had had *no idea* . . . what must Miss Eyre think of her interrupting like this, it was quite unpardonable, she would not *dream* of troubling her now . . .

'Come in, Miss Foxe,' said Leonora impatiently. 'Have you met Mr Boyce? Humphrey, this is Miss Foxe who has the flat at the top of the house. Is there anything wrong, Miss Foxe?'

'Only that the water is coming through my ceiling,' she replied, 'but it is nothing, really.'

'Oh, is it raining?' Leonora glanced towards the window. The hot day had broken in thunder without her having realised it; so much for the power of love, or lust, as one might well call it. 'Yes, so it is. Well, now, what can we do?'

'I thought perhaps if you had a bucket . . .,' Miss Foxe began.

'A *bucket*?' Leonora echoed. Really, did one look the sort of person who would have a bucket?

'Something to catch the water in,' suggested Humphrey, amused at the ideas of two gentlewomen without buckets. 'Let's go up and see, if Miss Foxe doesn't mind.'

They followed her up the stairs and into her sitting-room. Humphrey noticed one or two good pieces of furniture and china and made a mental note of them. The rain was dripping through a corner of the ceiling into a large Chinese vase.

'My dear Miss Foxe, that is quite a valuable piece,' he said.

'Is it valuable?' she asked casually. 'We had two of them at home – they used to stand in the drawing-room with pot-pourri in them. I believe a great-uncle brought them back from the East.'

'You have some charming things here,' said Humphrey, peering through the glass front of a corner cupboard. 'If you should ever feel the need to – er . . .' He did not like to go further.

'Mr Boyce is a dealer in antiques,' Leonora explained, 'and would give you the best advice if ever you wanted to sell anything.'

'Oh, I hope I shall never have to do that,' said Miss Foxe. 'I like to have my treasures around me. Why, it doesn't seem to be dripping so much now.'

'No, the rain has stopped,' said Humphrey. 'I tell you what I'll do,' he turned to Leonora, 'I'll send my builder round in the morning. He's a good man and won't overcharge you.'

'Oh, that *would* be kind,' said Miss Foxe rather too effusively, considering that it was for Leonora rather than her that the builder was being sent.

Humphrey and Leonora went down to her flat. There was still a little brandy left in his glass, but it was obvious that the evening had come to an end. Nothing was said about the scene that had preceded Miss Foxe's interruption, but Humphrey got the impression from Leonora's almost exaggeratedly cool and affected manner that he had made rather a fool of himself. She kissed him on the cheek as usual when they said goodnight and he reiterated his promise to send the builder round in the morning. Perhaps that practical deed would be more appropriate than some too carefully chosen object or a rather obvious sheaf of flowers. And anyway, what had he done that he should apologise to her? Only shown that he found her attractive, and surely all women wanted that reassurance occasionally?

Leonora also dismissed the episode from her mind. Funny old Humphrey, it must have been the brandy. One really couldn't have him going on like that. Examining her dress she found that the material was not torn, only the stitching at the shoulder seam, and it could easily be repaired.

XII

Soon after the visit to the furniture depository Phoebe had occasion to go to London to buy carbons and a new typewriter ribbon, the outpourings of the journal she was editing having exhausted it to a pale, barely decipherable grey. As tea-time approached, though this was not an hour that registered itself in Phoebe's consciousness, she found herself near Sloane Square, walking in the direction of the antique shop. She had made a kind of plan to get into conversation with somebody—she hadn't got quite as far as imagining who this might be—in the hope of obtaining more recent news of James than his last postcard had given her.

There was nobody visible as she approached the window, but then she saw that a woman, with a white teacup in her hand, was lurking at the back.

'I'm so sorry,' she said, as Phoebe entered, 'I'm expecting Mr Boyce back at any minute. Perhaps I can help you?'

'I'm a friend of Mr Boyce's nephew,' said Phoebe boldly.

'Oh, then perhaps you'd like a cup of tea,' said Miss Caton with an air of relief. 'I was afraid you might be a potential buyer.'

Phoebe accepted the tea almost gratefully, though it

was horribly strong, for her wanderings had made her tired. Miss Caton was a kind old thing and very ready to chat. It was the easiest thing in the world for Phoebe to ask casually if she knew Miss Eyre, who had packed up James's furniture for him.

'Oh, Miss Eyre,' she breathed, almost with reverence. 'She's a *great* friend of Mr Boyce's. Do you remember when we had the burglary? She sent flowers – wasn't that a lovely thing to do? And I happen to know,' here she paused rather coyly, 'Mr Boyce is taking her to Covent Garden tonight.'

So Miss Eyre was a friend of *Humphrey's* – that explained everything. What more natural than that she should supervise the packing up of James's furniture? She must be a sort of aunt to James. There was no time to glean any further information before Humphrey himself came into the shop, evidently annoyed about something. Phoebe noticed that Miss Caton whisked the teacups away very quickly, almost as if she didn't want him to see them.

'This is too bad!' he exclaimed. 'A wasted afternoon.'

Phoebe felt she ought to say something but he went on, apparently not noticing her, 'Lot 90 should have come up around three o'clock, but when I got there at ten to they'd reached Lot 105.'

'Oh dear, I wonder why that was,' murmured Miss Caton.

'Because some stupid woman had decided to withdraw her miserable things from the sale – "The Property of a Lady – withdrawn".'

'*This* young lady is a friend of Mr James's,' said Miss Caton, indicating Phoebe.

Humphrey looked startled. Phoebe's rather strange appearance did not appeal to him personally, but she was a woman and young. Ha! he said to himself, deliberately melodramatic, so young James has been keeping a mistress somewhere. What will Leonora say to *this*?

'You know James well?' he found himself asking.

'I met him some time ago at a party,' Phoebe explained. 'He sometimes comes to see me in the country – I'm working there at the moment.'

So that was how it was, thought Humphrey. Now he could admit to himself that he had always had some doubt as to the sex of James's lovers. Perhaps, as uncle and nephew, they had been in too close a relationship for James to confide in him. Or perhaps they had not been close enough. And this most decidedly *was* a girl. He had put on his spectacles to make quite sure, for it wasn't always easy to tell these days.

'My dear, I hope Miss Caton has been looking after you,' he said cordially. 'Perhaps you would care for a glass of sherry?'

'Well, thanks,' said Phoebe awkwardly.

'James writes very happily from Zaragoza,' Humphrey went on, giving the word a laboriously correct pronunciation, 'but of course you probably have more recent news of him.'

'Not really,' said Phoebe unhappily.

'The Spanish postal system is appalling and ours is not what it was,' said Humphrey smoothly. 'James will be going on to Portugal and then home. He seems to have picked up a companion on his travels.'

'Somebody who knows about antiques?' asked

98

Phoebe, trying to sound indifferent.

'He is "an American called Ned",' said Humphrey, 'so perhaps that's unlikely.'

Phoebe was only too relieved to learn that the companion was male, when it might so easily have been a girl.

'It must be rather lonely for him,' said Miss Caton chattily, 'like going on holiday by oneself. I always prefer to go with a party.'

'But James is not on holiday,' Humphrey reminded her. 'He is on a collecting tour and I hope he'll bring back something worth having.'

'I think I must go now,' said Phoebe. 'I've got to get to Putney where my mother lives. East Putney.'

'Ah, yes, you can get a train from Sloane Square, I believe,' said Humphrey with the vagueness of one who never uses public transport. 'Isn't that so, Miss Caton?'

'Oh yes,' said Miss Caton firmly. 'It's on the District Line.'

'You're sure of that?' asked Humphrey. 'It might be as well to inquire at the station.'

Phoebe, who knew perfectly well that East Putney could be reached from Sloane Square, went away feeling quite satisfied with her afternoon's work.

As Miss Caton had confided to Phoebe, Humphrey was taking Leonora to the opera that evening. It was not a form of entertainment he cared for overmuch, for he was unmusical, though he knew what he ought to like. Tonight it was *Tosca*, Leonora's favourite opera. Was her taste, her passion almost, for Puccini a little unworthy of her? Humphrey wondered. Was there just a hint of the second-rate about it and would he have admired her more if she had preferred Mozart? Yet it was this tiny flaw in her perfection that made her human and it was surely not unnatural that she should identify herself with the heroine. There must be few women, he supposed, who wouldn't claim to have lived for art and love. It was a pity that he had what might be an unpleasant piece of news for her. He could of course keep quiet about the girl who had visited the shop this afternoon, but he felt it was better that Leonora should know. And who better to tell her than himself?

Leonora was looking beautiful and remote in black lace. 'Such ravishing music,' she whispered, leaning towards Humphrey and allowing his sleeve to brush against her bare arm. She had evidently quite forgiven him for his silly behaviour the other evening and he had certainly made amends for it by asking his builder to call round the next day so that the leaking roof had been quickly repaired. That was the kind of thing one really wanted from somebody like Humphrey, Leonora thought, moving a little away from him.

Was *Tosca* the happiest of choices? he wondered, considering the news he had to break to her. While one could see Leonora as the heroine, living for art and love, it was difficult to imagine James and himself as Mario and Scarpia. He had never forced his attentions on her, Humphrey told himself, not without smugness; he had been content to wait until she should see fit to turn to him and now might be just such a time. When should he break the news to her and where? Not in the crush bar during the interval, for he had been looking forward to his drink all through the first act. And it would be cruel to upset Leonora in the second interval, with the tragic last act to follow. It would have to be when they were having supper.

'*Not* smoked Parma ham,' said Humphrey hastily as, some time later, they studied the menu. A colleague of his had had an unfortunate experience with it. A good hot soup might be best for both of them, but Leonora wanted an avocado pear filled with shrimps. Humphrey allowed her to take a mouthful and pronounce it delicious before embarking on his task.

'My dear,' he declared, 'I have a piece of news for you.'

'*News?* What can it be? Something nice?' she asked in a teasing voice.

'In a way – it depends how you look at it. I don't feel that "nice" is quite the word.'

'Not nice, then. Exciting? Amusing?'

'Yes, amusing, perhaps.' Really, he mustn't delay much longer. 'What do you think our young friend James has been up to?' he asked, deliberately more pompous than usual.

'Oh, it's about *James*.' Her manner seemed to alter. 'What has James been "up to", as you put it?'

'Keeping a mistress!' There, it was out. 'All this time he's had this girl tucked away in the country and we none of us knew about her.'

A shrimp fell on to the tablecloth, but perhaps it would have fallen anyway.

'How messily one eats,' said Leonora calmly. 'Is it a sign of age, or what? Shall I try to get the mayonnaise up with my knife?'

'Oh, leave it,' said Humphrey impatiently. 'Don't tell

me you knew all along about James?'

'Well, one had guessed *something*.' Leonora took a sip of Sauterne. 'After all, James is so beautiful – one always supposed that he must have *some* love life. Tell me how you found out.'

'This girl came to the shop, obviously wanting news of him.'

'Hadn't he written, then?'

'No doubt, but you know what posts are.'

'And one knows what dear James is – one would have thought *she* did. What's she like? Young? Pretty? Elegant?' Leonora tried to keep the eager curiosity out of her voice.

'Young – about twenty, I suppose. Rather badly dressed, with that droopy look girls seem to have now. Straggly long hair and a coat made of some sort of skin, leather, I think.'

'James always said he hated leather coats – it only goes to show something. And what's her name?'

'Phoebe Sharpe.'

Phoebe Sharpe,' Leonora murmured, and just as Jennifer had experienced a feeling of disquiet and distaste on hearing the name 'Leonora Eyre', so Leonora was conscious of a slight uneasiness now. The name evoked a memory of Gilbert and Sullivan (*The Yeoman of the Guard*?) and Thackeray's Becky Sharpe; a disturbing combination, but perhaps in the circumstances any name would have had its disagreeable undertones.

'I believe her mother lives in Putney – *East* Putney, I think she said.'

Leonora laughed. 'What an extraordinary picture you paint. It doesn't sound at all like James. Are you *sure?'*

'Oh, yes. She went to get a District Line train from Sloane Square after she left the shop.'

'I didn't doubt the part of Putney,' said Leonora. 'I meant, how could you be sure about their relationship?'

'I had the feeling – one can't really explain it. Anyway, don't all young people these days "sleep around" – if that's the expression?'

'I don't know,' said Leonora fastidiously. 'One hardly would know such things and one certainly doesn't attempt to keep up with modern slang. I seem to remember that people used to "sleep around", as you put it, twenty years ago and more.'

Humphrey looked rather crestfallen. 'So you aren't exactly astonished at my news?' he asked.

'About James? No, I'm not all that surprised, as I told you. And how does one know that he hasn't got entangled with a pretty Spanish girl by now?'

'That's rather what poor Miss Sharpe was afraid of, I suspect,' said Humphrey, relieved that Leonora was taking it so well.

In the taxi going home he was rather tender with her, as far as she would permit it, but she did not invite him in. Anyway, they would only have talked about James, he thought.

Leonora stood in the hall, waiting for the taxi to drive away. When lovely woman stoops to folly, she said to the fruitwood mirror with the cupids, though of course it wasn't exactly *that*. In the kitchen she thought she could almost 'fancy' a cup of strong Indian tea, but of course one couldn't really see oneself drinking tea after that delicious dinner. She was calm – perhaps numb with shock — for she had certainly had no idea that James was seeing another woman, whatever she may have pretended to Humphrey. Nevertheless she had been thinking ever since she heard the news and now she knew exactly what she was going to do. She undressed, hung up and folded her clothes methodically, then sat down at her desk in her night things and began to write a letter.

'Dear Miss Foxe,' it began. 'I am afraid I may have to ask you to vacate your flat at the end of the month instead of when the lease runs out, as we had arranged.' 'Arranged' was perhaps an exaggeration, for they had done no more than discuss the future in the vaguest terms and Leonora had found herself hoping, unworthily she knew, that Miss Foxe might not be fully aware of her strong position as the tenant of an unfurnished flat. And being of such gentle birth there was always the possibility that she might feel herself bound to do whatever Leonora wanted. Leonora continued, 'A friend of mine is coming back from abroad and has nowhere else to go, so I am sure you will appreciate the position.' Leonora paused again, seeing the 'friend' as Miss Foxe might imagine this person — a woman who had done some splendid service, nursing or in the mission field. 'Of course I shall do all I can to help you to find alternative accommodation' — that was the jargon, she believed — 'Yours very sincerely' — it was best to be very sincere in this sort of letter — 'Leonora M. Eyre.'

She would get in touch with the furniture depository in the morning — there was nothing more she could do now.

XIII

James was reading a letter from Leonora. The companion he had picked up on his travels ('an American called Ned') watched with a smile playing about his lips, as if he expected to have extracts from the letter read out to him.

'Well?' he asked, as James folded up the letter and put it back into the envelope.

'Nothing, really,' James mumbled.

'Come now, Jimmie, there must have been *something* in that letter to make you fold it up and put it away so quickly. You should've seen the look on your face . . .' Ned's thin gnat-like voice went on teasing and probing. He was small and neat, with smooth fair hair and blue eyes, appearing much younger than his twenty-nine years, until a closer look at his face revealed that life had, after all, left its mark.

They were in a hotel in Lisbon where they were spending some time before returning to London. Their room was cramped and sunless, yet stuffy in the hot afternoon, with no view but a long deep plunge into a well on to which the kitchen quarters opened. The clatter of dishes and bursts of unintelligible shouting could be heard as the hotel servants washed up or prepared some meal of the past or future.

James lay on one of the beds where he had been reading Leonora's letter. He was staring at the wall which was covered in a kind of striped paper, like the inside of an old-fashioned suitcase. One might almost be in a suitcase here, with the heat and the general feeling of constriction which Ned's presence and his whining American voice gave. Closing his eyes, James tried to imagine Leonora's cool green-walled room with the trailing plants and some delicious drink by his side. Her letter, with all its news of her doings, had brought her vividly before him. She had been going to *Tosca* with Humphrey on the day she wrote and would be wearing her black lace dress. And she had been scanning the papers and estate agents' windows to see if she could find him a suitable flat. ('After all, you won't want to be stuck with Humphrey for ever!') By the time he got back she hoped to have a list of suitable places for him to look at — wouldn't it be fun? Of course it would be, but James had rather wanted to do his own flat-hunting . . .

'Was it from Phoebe, that letter?' Ned went on relentlessly.

Phoebe. How remote Phoebe seemed now, as if she had never been. James felt a slight pang of conscience about her, for he had sent her only a few perfunctory postcards and not answered her last two letters. Ned thought it a waste of time to bother with letters when one was travelling, though he himself did write twice a week to his mother in Cambridge, Massachusetts.

'No, it was from Leonora,' James answered rather shortly.

'Leonora, your *elegant* friend . . .'

'Yes, you must meet her when you come to London,'

said James, trying to imagine the occasion and relieved that the meeting need not take place for a while, since Ned was staying with friends in Oxford before coming to work in the British Museum. He had a sabbatical year from the small respectable New England college where he was an assistant professor of English, during which time he hoped to complete his doctoral thesis.

'We'd have such a lot in common, I feel,' Ned went on in his most guileless manner. 'I just *love* elegant English ladies. Does she wear wide-brimmed hats and long narrow shoes?'

'She dresses very well,' said James, on the defensive. Indeed, Leonora's letter had included a description of some of the new autumn clothes she was having made — a lilac-coloured tweed coat and dress and 'yet another little black number, rather filmy and floating and suitable for feeling emotional in', as she put it. It was impossible to imagine Phoebe describing *her* clothes. Her last letter had been very different from Leonora's civilised account of life — a raw outpouring of feelings, full of references to things he wanted to forget, and running through it all the unspoken reproaches that made him feel so guilty. What an uncomfortable sort of girl Phoebe was and how badly he had behaved towards her!

'And can I meet Phoebe too?' Ned persisted.

'If you like. She's certainly very intelligent,' said James hopefully, realising that she and Ned might find a good deal to talk about. All the same, one couldn't quite see her, or any girl for that matter, falling in love with Ned.

'I suppose I'd have a lot in common with Phoebe, and

not only English literature,' said Ned, giving James a sideways look. 'You must bring us *all* together. How about having a cocktail party in your new apartment?'

'Yes, that's an idea,' said James, with forced heartiness. 'But of course I haven't *got* a new apartment yet.'

'Maybe not, but you will have. In the meantime, what are we waiting for?'

'I don't know,' said James.

Ned's scent, so much more powerful and exotic than the discreetly British 'after-shave' which was all that James had ever used, seemed to fill the room as he came nearer to the bed where James was lying still holding Leonora's letter in his hand.

XIV

Getting rid of Miss Foxe proved surprisingly easy. Leonora had left the letter for her on the table in the hall where she could not fail to see it, rather than risk the embarrassment of an encounter by slipping it under her door. She had then gone out to calm herself and prepare for what was to come, for even Leonora – hard though she professed to be – could not but realise that turning an elderly gentlewoman out of her home might well be an upsetting experience. She paced round the park in the sunshine, admiring the beds of heliotrope and fuchsia and remembering the time she had walked there with James. It was for him that she was doing this, not for herself. Two turns round the park convinced her of the rightness of her action, so that when she got back to the house to find Miss Foxe hovering in the hall she was ready for her, determined to be firm but not unkind, or at least no more unkind than was necessary.

'Oh, Miss Eyre,' said Miss Foxe – they had never become 'Leonora' and 'Charlotte' to each other – 'I've just had your letter. I wonder if we could talk about it.'

'Certainly, Miss Foxe,' said Leonora, relieved that she did not appear unduly agitated. 'Come in and have a cup of coffee,' she added graciously.

'Oh, thank you, Miss Eyre, your coffee is always *so* delicious.'

'I'm afraid my letter must have been rather a shock to you,' Leonora began as she poured the coffee.

'Well, in a way it was, but really it was more of a relief. You see, I've been wanting to ask you if I could leave before the end of the lease, because I've found what I believe one calls "alternative accommodation" '—here they smiled at each other—'and naturally I'm anxious to get into it as soon as possible.'

Leonora was almost disappointed. Where could Miss Foxe have found to go at as reasonable a rent as her present one that would be at all suitable?

'It's St Basil's Priory,' Miss Foxe went on, as if Leonora would know at once what she meant. 'A delightful country house for elderly people run by Anglican nuns,' she explained, 'and they've agreed to take me in.'

She made herself sound like a fallen woman, Leonora thought, being 'taken in' by nuns.

'A vacancy occurred through death—Mrs Ainger told me about it, only of course you don't know her, do you?—anyway, there it is and I should like to go next week.'

'But what about your furniture?' Leonora asked, thinking of Humphrey. 'I suppose you'll want to sell it?'

'Oh, no, I can take my bits and pieces with me. I'm to have two unfurnished rooms.'

'I see—it sounds ideal for you.'

'Yes, I'm so glad things have turned out like this. When you said that in your note about your friend returning from abroad and needing somewhere to live, I thought, well, perhaps this has somehow been *arranged*, you know . . .'She inclined her head upwards in the direction of the ceiling, 'I do believe things sometimes *are*, Miss Eyre . . .'

Perhaps this really *had* been, thought Leonora, with James in mind.

'And there's central heating, so no more bother with those heavy paraffin cans and wondering if the man is going to call. I always remember how kind your nephew was that time, taking it all the way upstairs for me. I think of that kind action when we hear about all this hooliganism and violence everywhere – young people aren't *all* like that, are they?'

Leonora was disconcerted for a moment – surely James, her 'nephew', didn't appear to be as young as all that? And yet if he did, so much the better. 'Have you fixed with the removal men?' she asked. 'I know a very good firm.'

'Oh, that's all settled,' said Miss Foxe eagerly. 'Two of the lay brothers will come with the van.'

Leonora expressed astonishment.

'Yes, you see there are monks as well – oh, not living all together, of course, but quite near. And they help the sisters with all kinds of little jobs. In fact one of the lay brothers was a remover's man before he entered St Basil's.'

'How strange,' said Leonora. It was certainly a convenient arrangement but she did hope that the lay brothers and their van wouldn't be too conspicuous in the road and make the whole operation ridiculous, or offend in any way against her own dignity.

When the moving day came, Leonora was of course woman enough to watch from the shadow of her curtains. One of the lay brothers was strikingly good-looking, really such a waste, one felt, while the other, perhaps the one who had been a furniture remover in his worldly life, was short and stockily built. Leonora watched Miss Foxe's things being taken down to the van, noticing particularly the Chinese jars which Humphrey had coveted. When everything had been loaded up Leonora made her appearance in the hall to say good bye. She could afford to be gracious now and was at her most charming, wishing Miss Foxe all happiness in her new life. It was perhaps regrettable that Miss Foxe was to travel down in the van with the brothers, and the three of them looked rather odd perched up in front, Miss Foxe in the middle. Still, she had gone, that was the main thing. The house would be very different now.

Leonora could not resist running up into the empty flat and imagining James's things arranged in the rooms, for now she could freely admit to herself that it was her intention to have him living under her roof. The events that had led up to this decision, and the anxiety, almost unhappiness, had been pushed into the back of her mind by the business of Miss Foxe's removal. Now she began to go over what Humphrey had said and wonder how seriously she ought to take it and what she could do about it. From Humphrey's description of the girl it all sounded rather sordid and unworthy, the kind of liaison James would be ashamed of and that meant very little to him. For nothing could touch *their* relationship, their rare and wonderful friendship, Leonora was sure of that.

All the same she was curious about the girl. She knew that James had been going to lend a few bits of his furniture to a friend in the country, but had thought nothing of it at the time. Could the friend be this girl, Phoebe Sharpe? It would be easy to find out when she arranged about getting James's furniture moved into the empty flat. After all, it would save the cost of storage to have his things in her house and he could choose his own decorations when he came back.

The foreman at the depository was most helpful — Leonora had already classified him as a 'sweet little man' — and was able to give her the address of the young lady who had arranged for the furniture to be sent to her in the country. And of course the name was Miss Sharpe.

Now there was the question of what to do next. Should she write and announce herself or call unexpectedly — people in the country were always in — and thus see for herself the scene of James's crime, if one could call it that? Leonora of course had no car, nor did she wish to enlist Humphrey's help on this occasion; she wanted to go alone, to arrive anonymously by train or bus. There was something pleasingly adventurous about a journey by Green Line bus, and by a fortunate coincidence it seemed that one passed through the village. Once she got there it should be easy to find Vine Cottage.

Leonora was the only person getting out of the bus in the village. It was the middle of the afternoon, hot and sunny, and the place was deserted as if one were in Italy or Spain and the inhabitants were having their siesta.

She could not see anybody to ask the way so she began to walk slowly down the wide main street until she came to the church. Then, seeing what looked like a cottage through the trees, she turned towards it and came upon a gate with the name Vine Cottage on a faded wooden plaque.

So this was it. Seen through Leonora's eyes it looked shabby, almost mean, not the kind of place she would have chosen to live in herself. Yet the shady front garden and the little windows overgrown with climbing roses suggested an ideal setting for a love affair, and she found that she was trembling and had to pause with her hand on the gate to think what she would do first. She would announce herself, saying that she was the friend of James's who had packed up his furniture and that he was coming back soon and would need it. After that she would see how things went.

There was a tarnished brass knocker in the form of a dolphin on the front door. What a pity Miss Sharpe didn't clean it, Leonora thought, as she lifted it and knocked. And surely something could have been done to the front garden? Presumably the vine was round at the back for there was no trace of it here. 'I am Leonora Eyre,' she said to herself as she waited, and the declaration gave her courage and a feeling of security. After a while she knocked again but there was still no answer. She pushed against the door and it opened. How careless people were in the country, she thought, noticing that all the windows were open too; they seemed to have no fear of burglars or intruders.

She found herself in a small low-ceilinged room, dark and cool after the sunshine outside and extremely untidy.

'Is anybody in?' she called out tentatively, for Miss Sharpe might be upstairs or out at the back. But there was no answer. Leonora sat down, for she was very tired. Perhaps she had even hoped to be offered a cup of tea, though given the circumstances of her visit that was perhaps unlikely. Also the general appearance of the room suggested nothing so conventional. Most of the space was taken up by a round table on which stood a typewriter, stacks of books, papers and letters, a pile of roughly dried washing, and the remains of a meal — a loaf, cheese, butter, and a mug half full of a brownish liquid. In the middle of it all was a tabby and white cat, curled up asleep. Along one wall was a sofa heaped with brightly coloured cushions, gramophone records and more books. It was difficult, impossible really, to imagine James in such a setting and Leonora began to go over the evidence she had — apart from his furniture of which there was no sign — for supposing that there was anything between James and Phoebe Sharpe. It was true that Phoebe had been to Humphrey's shop and spoken of James as her friend, but perhaps Humphrey had jumped to the wrong conclusions. She decided to withhold an opinion until she had seen the girl.

Leonora stood up and looked around her. A lamp made out of a wine bottle caught her eye and she smiled, remembering that James had once had one until she had gently teased him into putting it away. There were no pictures or objects to give any clue to Phoebe Sharpe's tastes, except possibly the books. Leonora opened one of them — it was poetry, but without her glasses she could make nothing of it. A place in it had been marked by an envelope addressed in James's unmistakable large sprawling hand, she didn't need her glasses to recognise *that*. It gave her a shock to see a letter from him addressed to somebody else and she stood with it in her hand, wondering if she should open it. Of course one didn't read other people's letters, one wasn't that kind of person, but in the circumstances, and bearing in mind the close relationship between herself and James, going against one's better nature though it would be . . .

There was a light tap on the door. Leonora quickly replaced the letter in the book and arranged herself in an attitude of waiting, realising that it could hardly be Phoebe knocking on her own door.

'Oh . . . is Miss Sharpe not here?' A tall fair woman of about Leonora's own age came into the room.

Leonora stood up and the two women confronted each other.

'I came to see her too, but there seems to be nobody here,' she explained. 'I am Leonora Eyre,' she announced, making the declaration that was to have given her confidence for the encounter with Phoebe.

'And I am Rose Culver,' countered the woman, almost challenging her.

Leonora took up the challenge by a cool appraisal of the woman's clothes — cotton dress, bare legs and canvas sandals — did one have to dress like that in the country? Nevertheless Miss Culver had her own kind of distinction even if only that of a typical English spinster.

'A friend of mine lent Miss Sharpe some furniture,' she explained, 'and I came to see her about returning it. I'm furnishing a flat for him and he'll need the things.'

'You came all this way to ask her that?' asked Miss

Culver, as if she found it strange, 'Wouldn't it have been better to write or telephone first?'

Leonora was not used to having her actions questioned or criticised and was about to return a sharp answer when Miss Culver appeared to soften, remarking on the heat of the afternoon and inviting Leonora to have tea at her own cottage.

'That's very kind . . .,' Leonora hesitated, ' . . . do you think Miss Sharpe will be back this afternoon?'

'She's probably gone to London for the day. Would you like to leave a note for her?'

'No, I think I'll write when I get home.' Things had hardly turned out as Leonora had expected and the next step was not clear. Leonora could not of course confide in Miss Culver, but she was in great need of tea and allowed herself to be led into the next-door cottage, shown where to 'wash her hands', given an embroidered guest towel, and then placed in a deckchair with a canopy and footstool in a delightful little garden. She was even asked if she preferred Earl Grey or Darjeeling.

Leonora leaned back and closed her eyes. The country was certainly most agreeable in some ways and Miss Culver seemed a nice woman. Perhaps after all it had been a good thing that Phoebe Sharpe had been out; it was much more dignified never to meet her, and after seeing the state of that room Leonora felt she hardly wished to.

Miss Culver poured tea and handed the thinnest of brown bread and butter.

'Delicious,' murmured Leonora, 'you're so kind.' After her second cup of tea she inquired tentatively whether Miss Culver had ever met James.

'Oh, there seem to be several young people who come to see Phoebe Sharpe,' said Miss Culver vaguely. 'I can't say that I know any of them by name.'

Leonora found this encouraging and was conscious of a feeling of relief; perhaps James was only one of many. 'He is a very great friend of mine,' she said, 'we're very close.'

'The odd thing about men is that one never really knows,' said Miss Culver, 'Just when you think they're close they suddenly go off.'

Leonora was startled and wondered if she had heard correctly. For a moment the two ageing unmarried women looked at each other in a way that seemed to ask, 'What can *you* know of being close to a man?' It was a temporary embarrassment, however. Leonora quickly recovered, deciding that Miss Culver was obviously one of those eccentric women who live alone and don't always realise what they are saying.

'What a delightful herb garden,' she remarked. 'I've never seen such marvellous parsley.'

'Yes, it does seem to flourish here — would you like some?'

'Thank you, I should. And I think perhaps I ought to be going for my bus.'

'Ah, yes, you'll want to get the four forty-five — it won't be crowded in the middle of the week, but I always like to be in plenty of time myself. I'll come and show you where the stop is.'

How completely dull and normal Miss Culver appeared now, as they walked along together, Leonora carrying her bunch of parsley with such elegance that it looked like an exotic accessory to her outfit. In the bus she brooded a little over that unexpected remark about men 'going off' just when you thought they were close. She hardly liked to admit it, but she did sometimes feel slightly uneasy when James was out of her sight and this business with Phoebe Sharpe — whether there had been much or little in it — showed that her anxiety was justified. Not that one thought of James as 'men', of course, or regarded him quite as other people. It wasn't as if one could *marry* James, for instance, though it was amusing to toy with the idea. 'Quietly in London', one sometimes read, perhaps even 'very quietly'. Surely life — and literature — were not without precedents for such a marriage? Then she remembered Humphrey looming over her that evening, but of course dear James wouldn't expect anything like *that* . . .

When she got home she wrote a note to Phoebe about the furniture, explaining that it would now be needed and suggesting a time when it might be collected, a few cool but polite lines that would no doubt have the desired effect.

XV

Three days later Leonora was in an antique shop in Kensington Church Street, examining a pair of porcelain vases.

'They're quite perfect, Madam,' said the woman assistant coldly. 'You won't find any flaw, I can assure you.'

'That may be,' said Leonora, equally cold, 'but one likes to see for oneself.' They had certainly looked perfect that evening when she and James had walked past the shop and he had admired them so, but Humphrey had impressed on her the importance of making quite sure. 'What are you asking for them?' she inquired, her voice becoming a degree colder.

The woman, very clear and cool, stated the price.

Leonora repeated this on a questioning note, as if she could hardly believe what she had just been told.

'That *is* the price, Madam.'

The temperature of the little room now fell to zero, although it was a warm September afternoon outside. An icy silence lay between the two women.

'Very well then, I'll take them.' One did not haggle of course, Leonora told herself, and the faint doubt in her mind was not whether these beautiful objects were too expensive but whether it was entirely wise to spend *quite* so much money on James's birthday present. Still, it wasn't as if she didn't like them herself; they were exquisite and as James was coming to live in her house they would, in a sense, be hers too. She sat down at a little table, also exquisite in its humbler way, and began to write out the cheque.

The woman hovered over her, almost smiling. 'May we send them somewhere for you, Madam?' she asked.

'Thank you, no.' Leonora almost smiled too. 'I have a taxi waiting outside, so if you could just pack them up in something . . .'

'With pleasure, Madam.'

Leonora drew on her long lilac-coloured gloves while the woman busied herself with shavings and tissue paper and a large box. When she had finished she came out to the taxi and handed the parcel in.

'How beautifully packed, thank you *so* much.' Leonora almost beamed. Somewhere from the back of her mind a ridiculous tag or motto had come to her, the sort of thing one saw, or rather had seen, in poker-work — something about passing through this world but once and therefore taking care to be kind to a fellow creature, which was absurd really, because she might well visit the shop again. Why had the woman called her 'Madam' so unnecessarily after every sentence, Leonora wondered, when she was obviously a social equal? Perhaps that was why. Does one then seem so cold, proud and formidable, she asked herself, when one is none of these things?

'Couldn't wait here much longer, Miss,' said the taxi

driver, grudgingly, but sure of a good tip.

'No, I *know*,' said Leonora warmly, 'it *was* good of you.' She leaned back with a sigh of relief, cradling the precious parcel in her arms.

When she got home there was some post lying in the hall. A card from James from Lisbon – Black Horse Square – with a loving message and looking forward to seeing her soon, and a letter in a cheap brown envelope, addressed in a small spiky hand and with the stamps stuck crookedly down one side. Not the sort of letter one was accustomed to receive, thought Leonora, wondering who it could be from.

'Dear Miss Eyre,' she read, 'I had your letter about James's furniture and it is certainly *not* convenient for it to be collected on Monday or at any time. I have no intention of giving up the things until James asks me to. Yours sincerely, P. J. Sharpe.'

It was some seconds before Leonora realised that the anonymous, even masculine-sounding 'P. J. Sharpe' was the girl Phoebe Sharpe, but of course the message about the furniture was clear enough. How upsetting and tiresome it all was! And what was she to do now, when James's other furniture had already come from the depository and been arranged in the flat upstairs. It was too bad, and almost took away the pleasure which buying the vases had given her. Perhaps Humphrey could suggest something. It was half-past three; Leonora decided to summon him to tea with her.

Humphrey was in the act of selling a pair of Staffordshire figures to an exacting Jewess from Brondesbury when Miss Caton came hovering in the background with 'an urgent telephone call from Miss

Eyre'. Humphrey excused himself and went to the telephone, but in the two minutes he was away the potential buyer had changed her mind, and the American woman who had been 'just looking around' had suddenly remembered that she had arranged to meet her husband in twenty minutes' time at the Hilton and couldn't decide right now whether she really wanted the bronze representing Actaeon set upon by hounds.

Not that one really *needed* to sell things, Humphrey told himself as he got into his car, and poor Leonora had sounded genuinely distressed. Yet it did seem rather a storm in a teacup or whatever was the appropriate phrase, all this fuss about James's few sticks of furniture. He could lend him a few of the less choice pieces from the shop, if necessary — but if Leonora was unhappy something must be done about it.

'But, my dear, this is monstrous — that *you* should be worried about James's bits and pieces,' he fulminated, as they sat in Leonora's little patio drinking tea.

'I wanted to have everything nice for him when he got back,' Leonora faltered, on the edge of tears.

'I know you did, my love,' said Humphrey at his most soothing, 'and you shall. We'll drive down there now and bring the stuff back with us.'

'*Now?*'

'Why not? It's only quarter past four — we can be down there by six.'

'But it's so sudden — I don't think I could face it at the end of a day.'

'You needn't do anything — you can sit in the car and wait, *I'll* go in and fetch them.'

'Very well then, I'll get ready.' Leonora went to her

bedroom and put on a mauve tweed coat; a black chiffon scarf draped gracefully over her head and dark glasses completed her outfit. At the last minute she slipped a bottle of smelling salts into her bag – one never knew, there *might* be unpleasantness.

Humphrey meanwhile was clearing the back of the estate car, removing a broken picture frame and a marble head, a few old copies of *The Times* and an umbrella, the sort of clutter that might give some indication of his trade. The sooner this business was settled the better, he thought. Get the furniture away from this girl and into Leonora's house and then let things take their course. He had been somewhat dismayed at Leonora's sudden, and to him rash, action in having James's furniture moved into her house. And was it really wise to go now and snatch back the things James had lent to his mistress – for this was how Humphrey now regarded Phoebe – without giving her due warning? Yet at the back of his mind there was a kind of hope, unworthy though he knew it to be, that this time Leonora might well have gone too far. And if James rebelled and left her, what would she do then? What *could* she do, but turn from the nephew to the much more suitable uncle?

There seemed to be something about the atmosphere of Vine Cottage that made people want to establish their identities so that there could be no doubt as to who they were. As Leonora and Miss Culver had declared themselves, so now Humphrey although they had already met at the shop, stood before Phoebe and announced; 'I am James's uncle.'

'Oh ...' Her startled face suggested that she feared bad news. Something had happened to James – he was dead, killed in a car or plane crash. She waited apprehensively.

'I wondered if I might collect those few small pieces of furniture he lent you.'

So James was not dead; not even her pride could be saved now.

'Oh, take them,' she said roughly. 'Did Miss Eyre send you here?'

'I offered to collect them,' said Humphrey more coldly. 'I am James's uncle,' he repeated, as if it were a magic formula, 'if you would kindly show me ...'

'There's this chair, and a little table upstairs.'

He followed her up, embarrassed at entering what was obviously her bedroom. With an angry gesture Phoebe swept a pile of books off the table. 'That's the table,' she said, 'and there's one or two other things. ...' Humphrey picked up the table. It was not heavy but awkward to carry down the narrow staircase. Phoebe did not attempt to help him, but stood in the doorway, looking at the woman in the car. She knew immediately that it was Leonora Eyre – this cool elegant figure in mauve, her hair swathed in black chiffon. Her eyes were hidden by dark glasses but there was a glimpse of a pale cheek and a well-shaped mouth. This was certainly not the comfortable, grey-haired, motherly woman she had first imagined packing up James's things, nor even the aunt-like person she had been led to expect from Miss Caton's description. Seeing Leonora – one could hardly say meeting her – opened up to Phoebe a new dimension in James's life. A romantic attachment to an older woman; it explained a lot. In her scorn she classified Leonora as a mother figure to replace the one he had lost—what the girl in the photograph might have become if she had lived. She found herself wondering if James and Leonora ever made love together, but the idea was too distasteful to contemplate. No doubt the marble cheek would lean itself to be kissed, and perhaps that was enough for James.

The car drove off. Humphrey attempted a mollificatory wave in Phoebe's direction—he felt sorry for the girl—but Leonora remained still, her head turned away. Of course she had taken a surreptitious peep at Phoebe—no woman could have resisted that—but in her moment of triumph she preferred not to look upon the girl she now regarded as her vanquished rival.

XVI

'But, Jimmie, is that *wise*?' Anxiety seemed to intensify the gnat-like quality of Ned's voice, so that combined with the noise of the plane James really did feel as if an insect were buzzing round his head.

'It isn't a question of its being *wise*,' he said rather crossly. Wisdom was somehow the last quality one would associate with Ned, anyway. 'It just happens to be a convenient arrangement until I find myself a new flat. After all, I've got to live somewhere.'

'But with Leonora, and in the same *house* . . . Jimmie, you'll have to be firm with her and not let her boss you. Believe me, it could be *very* difficult to get away. With your sweet nature you might feel yourself under an *obligation* to her, and then where would you be?'

James did not answer but turned his head to look out of the window. They were flying through an eiderdown of grey clouds, coming down into a wet English autumn day.

Ned's friends from Oxford were meeting him with their car at London Airport, so James made the cool rainy bus journey to Cromwell Road alone with his thoughts. He had bought a carton of duty-free cigarettes for Phoebe on the plane and intended to give them to her at the first opportunity. It wasn't a very personal present, he realised — perhaps he ought to have got her a pair of filigree earrings or a Portuguese tile — but it was too late to worry about that now. The sunless drive through the spoiled countryside laid a deep melancholy on him, as it must over returning travellers with lives less complicated than James's had now become. Ned, Leonora, Phoebe . . . the names came to him in that order — how was he going to fit them all in? Did he even want to? He had already more or less dropped Phoebe and if he did not get in touch with her to give her the cigarettes she might just fade out, as other girls had done. But could he do without Leonora?

Climbing down out of the bus he saw that Leonora was there to meet him, wearing a raincoat like the iridescent wing of some beautiful beetle. Caught unawares for a moment, her face looked worried, almost old, and he felt a pang of love and pity for her.

'James!' She had seen him and was radiant. It was flattering and disturbing to think that the sight of him could bring about such a change. 'I've got a car waiting outside, so we can go straight home.'

Not even an ordinary taxi but a car hired specially to meet him.

Home, he thought, picturing his old flat with all his things around him. But home now was the flat at the top of Leonora's house where Miss Foxe had lived, whose rooms he had never entered. No doubt it had not been 'wise', but what could he have done to stop it? And anyway, as he had told Ned, it was only a temporary measure.

'You'll see that it needs redecorating,' Leonora

warned him as they went up, 'but of course I left it for you to choose what you want.'

'It's lovely,' said James weakly.

It was certainly better than he had imagined and Leonora had done one of her marvellous flower arrangements of chrysanthemums and michaelmas daisies in the sitting-room.

'Oh, it's so wonderful to have you back!' Leonora came up to him impulsively and flung her arms around him. James returned her embrace and for a moment they stood locked together in mutual pleasure at being reunited. Then James's attention wandered and he found himself looking towards the window, with its view of trees and roof-tops.

'Why, it's got bars on it,' he said.

'Yes, darling – I suppose it must have been the nursery once. I never noticed them before, though goodness knows one needed bars with poor Miss Foxe up here – one never knew *what* she might do. I can have them taken away if you feel fenced in,' she teased.

James laughed a little uncertainly.

'You'll be absolutely independent, you know,' Leonora went on. 'The man's coming to fix the telephone tomorrow so we shan't even be able to listen in to each other's calls.'

'I suppose you'll have to give me a rent book,' said James, half joking.

'Oh, I think an impersonal banker's order or something like that – don't you? One would be so embarrassed – one hardly likes to take your money as it is. I asked Humphrey what he thought the rent should be. Of course Miss Foxe was a controlled tenant.'

'Whereas I'm an uncontrolled one?'

'Absolutely, darling!'

They moved into the bedroom.

'*More* flowers,' said James, 'you *have* done things beautifully.'

'Yes, I thought just a discreet vase of late roses by the bed.'

Was there a hint of irony in Leonora's tone? James pondered uneasily over the possible significance of the roses, for she lacked Phoebe's directness. Then he saw the bedside table.

'But that's the little table I lent to somebody!' he exclaimed. 'Or I thought I'd lent it.'

'You did – but it came back,' said Leonora, in a cool amused tone.

'Oh, but I didn't mean . . .' What *had* he meant?

'I thought you should have it, so Humphrey and I went and got it.'

James sat down on the bed, defeated.

'Oh, don't look like that, my love. It didn't *matter* – can't you see that?'

James bowed his head before the horror of Leonora's unspoken forgiveness. He could not bring himself to ask if she and Phoebe had actually met and his imagination boggled at the idea of it.

'I thought perhaps a cold meal, but I've made one of *my* soups,' Leonora was saying, 'just for your first evening back. Then Humphrey wants us to go round for coffee and drinks. But first let me show you your *own* little kitchen, where you'll be cooking all those delicious Robert Carrier meals.'

*

The next day James was back in the shop. Everything seemed reassuringly yet depressingly the same. The sale rooms had not yet reopened after the summer recess and the only excitement was in the expectation of potential buyers from the people who passed the shop and loitered by the window.

James had crept quietly down from his flat that morning so as not to disturb Leonora, but there had been no sign of her. The unworthy thought occurred to him that perhaps she was not at her best in the early morning. Only a young girl could appear to advantage in a housecoat, with tousled hair and the sleep still in her eyes. But Phoebe had looked the same always, he remembered, except at those times when she came to London and made her rather pathetic efforts to appear suitably dressed.

'There's a parcel for you,' said Miss Caton brightly.

She had taken her summer holiday late and her leathery skin was still burnt an unbecoming brickish red. Now, when she brought the mid-morning instant coffee, still in the shameful thick white cups, she was obviously bursting to tell James all about it.

But he was preoccupied and inattentive, remembering that tomorrow was his birthday and suspecting that the parcel was from Phoebe.

It was a book – an anthology of modern poetry – so who else could it be from? There was no card or message to indicate the sender. James dared not look into the pages, fearing that he might come upon something to upset him.

'A book, is it?' asked Miss Caton. 'Oh, poetry,' she added in a falling tone. 'Mr Boyce said he wouldn't be coming in today. Nothing doing in the sale rooms, of course. There's been an American lady after that bronze – she might come in again. Mr Boyce said you could deal with her. It seems she can't make up her mind.'

'Tell me about your holiday, Miss Caton,' said James, who felt disinclined for work. 'You said you'd been on a coach tour? That must have been ·very interesting. Where did you go?'

Miss Caton drew a deep breath and began to tell him. James only half listened, making an occasional appropriate comment, but after a while there was something almost enjoyable about her tediously detailed account of the flight to Paris, the coach journey through France and Switzerland and the arrival at Lake Maggiore. Her friend's upset stomach and dislike of Continental Catholicism were made vivid to James, so that he found himself sharing in their relief at the eventual return to good plain food and the Anglican Church.

When evening approached James began to picture himself returning to the flat in Leonora's house and cooking a meal in the little kitchen. The next day, being his birthday, he would of course be dining with her, but what was he going to eat *now*? Should he buy food and take it home – grill a piece of steak or heat up a frozen pizza? It would obviously be difficult to make curry or fry onions or fish, for it was unthinkable that such smells should be permitted to waft down Leonora's elegant staircase. In the end it seemed easiest to have a meal out and go to a film, creeping quietly in at eleven o'clock so as not to disturb Leonora if she had already gone to bed. Should he perhaps tap on her sitting-room door to say goodnight? It would be pleasant to drink a cup of China tea with her. But just as he approached the door the sound of laughter came at him and the voice of Leonora's friend Liz, witty and cruel, saying, 'But, darling, one would hardly wish to be a mother to somebody like *that*!'

What and who could they have been talking about? James wondered. Surely not himself? He felt shut out from their feminine cosiness and a little annoyed that Leonora should be keeping so *very* much to herself.

The next evening, of course, things were quite different. While Leonora was busy in the kitchen James sat at the white wrought-iron table in her little patio, trying to write a letter to Phoebe. He must thank her for the anonymous book, suggest a meeting, do something to ease his conscience. And then there was that carton of cigarettes he had brought for her. Idly he sat staring at the flowers which surely went on flowering later for Leonora than for anyone else – begonias and dahlias and a second blossoming of roses. He wondered if the grapes at Vine Cottage had started to ripen yet or if they were of the kind that never could.

There was a movement behind him and Leonora was standing at his side with a drink in her hand. She was wearing a black dress of a kind of pleated material, chiffon he thought, and her newly done hair was curving smoothly on to her cheeks in a style rather too young for her but becoming enough in the failing light.

'Almost too dark to see,' she said, 'and I've brought you something with gin in it.'

James had automatically laid his arm over the sheet of paper which was so far virgin except for the date and the beginning, 'My dearest Phoebe'.

'A difficult letter?' Leonora asked in her most sympathetic tone.

He sighed. 'An impossible one, really.'

'Yes, some letters do seem to be that, don't they? And what a shame you should have to be writing letters on your birthday—surely tomorrow will do?'

James murmured something.

'Perhaps this one isn't really necessary,' Leonora went on. 'Silence is sometimes best, you know.'

'Yes, I suppose it is.' He would leave it for now, anyway. If Phoebe loved him she would understand, and if she didn't what did it matter? He crumpled up the page and put it in his pocket. Better, perhaps, not to leave it lying around.

'Are we ready to start the birthday celebrations, then?'

'Yes, let's.' James got up and they went into the house together.

'Here's your present—I do hope you'll like it.'

Leonora's air of sparkling excitement communicated itself to him as he undid the wrappings. And then there they stood, those exquisite objects he had admired in the shop window that evening when he had walked past with Phoebe, and of course on an earlier occasion with Leonora.

'You're so much too good to me—I just don't know how to thank you,' he said after a pause.

'Just give me a dutiful kiss,' said Leonora lightly.

He bent to kiss her cheek, his hands touching her

stiffly lacquered hair, the feeling of which gave him a slight shock as if she were made of some brittle unreal substance. 'Darling,' he said, 'they're so beautiful. Did Humphrey go with you to buy them?'

'No—I wanted it to be our secret,' she said. 'You know how it is with dear Humphrey. One wouldn't wish to be disloyal, of course, but he's *so* obsessed with trying to knock down the price of everything—being a dealer himself, I suppose—one sometimes finds it a *little* embarrassing.'

And of course he probably knew the owner of the shop anyway, James thought. It was almost frightening to realise that Leonora was willing to spend so much money on his birthday present. For now that he saw the vases again he felt that perhaps after all he didn't like them as much as he had remembered. There was something sickly in their colouring and over-elaborate in their design. Looking at them he felt like somebody—a child, of course—who has eaten too many cream cakes or whatever would be the equivalent nowadays. Saddened, he sat down at the table and prepared to enjoy his delicious birthday dinner.

XVII

'Hello, Jimmie—guess who!'

'Ned, of course,' said James in a rather subdued voice, for his uncle was in the shop and the telephone call had interrupted a lecture Humphrey had been giving his nephew on the advisability of settling down to serious study of some particular aspect of the antique trade.

'I know one learns a good deal by going round the sale rooms,' he said, 'but you should try to specialise in something—bronzes or porcelain or even furniture —*not* netsuke, I think,' he added, perhaps remembering his visits to Mr Lambe, the dentist.

James had just been going to say 'porcelain', in view of Leonora's birthday present to him, when the telephone had rung.

'See who that is,' said Humphrey crossly. 'If it's Mrs Hirschberg about that bronze, I'll speak to her.'

'Are you busy?' Ned asked.

'Yes, in a way,' said James cautiously.

'Okay, I'll make it short then. I'm coming up to the British Museum for a few days, so I'll look in on you at the weekend.'

'Oh, but . . .' James was confused, both by his uncle's presence and by the idea of Ned calling to see him at Leonora's house.

'You'll be away?'

'Possibly—can I let you know?'

'No time for that and I'm not sure where I'll be—I'll just take a chance. If you're there, I'll see you—if not, not. That sounds beautifully simple, doesn't it, Jimmie?'

'Yes, simple. I must rush off now.' But was anything about Ned 'simple'?

'Who was that—your girl friend?' asked Humphrey without much interest. 'I hope you've made it all right with her about that furniture. I didn't like having to snatch it away so unceremoniously, but Leonora was upset and seemed to think you'd want it and you know what she is—women do fuss so,' he added, but without disloyalty since it was a generalisation.

'Yes, they do,' James agreed. All the same, Leonora was being marvellous and he had settled down very comfortably in the flat. He had been afraid she would be always in and out wanting to know what he was doing but she didn't bother him at all. Occasionally when he came back in the evening he noticed that fresh flowers had appeared in his sitting-room, and of course she always saw that his milk was put in the fridge and his rubbish emptied and all those practical things that helped to make life run smoothly but that one didn't want to have to think about oneself.

Tonight *she* was dining with *him* and James hurried back, remembering to call at Harrods on the way for some of Leonora's favourite lemon water-ice. He spent some time arranging the flowers, not quite as artistically as she would have done them, he felt. Then he had to 'arrange' himself and was only just ready when she tapped on his door.

'Not too early, I hope?' she said.

'As if you could ever be.'

If the compliment was a little too glib Leonora gave no sign of noticing. 'I'd intended to be just a fashionable few minutes late,' she admitted.

'I'm glad you weren't—I've been longing to see you,' he said, and really it was true. He was much more at ease with her than with Phoebe or even Ned.

It was almost as if they were meeting for the first time or in the very early days of their knowing each other, Leonora felt with delight. All that wretched business about Phoebe Sharpe and the furniture seemed like a kind of nightmare, if that wasn't putting it too strongly. When the evening had advanced some way she planned to say just a *little* about Phoebe, to clear things up as it were. The position was not entirely satisfactory—the episode needed just a few touches to tidy it up before it was put away for ever.

'Lemon water-ice—*clever* James!'

'I was terrified it was all going to melt before I could get it home.'

She was touched to think of him going to so much trouble, when of course she could perfectly well have phoned Harrods to deliver it. Still, that wouldn't have been at all the same.

'Shall we draw the curtains to have our coffee?' he asked. 'Or would you like to sit in the gloaming with just one lamp on in the corner?'

'Oh, in the gloaming, I think. What a lovely word that is—do you suppose it's Anglo-Saxon or what?'

'I don't know, darling.'

'That clever friend of yours probably would—didn't you say she had a degree in English or something equally formidable?'

'You mean Phoebe Sharpe?' said James, frowning over the coffee percolator. He was puzzled that Leonora should appear to want to cast this shadow over what was being such a perfect evening.

'Yes, Phoebe Sharpe.'

'What about her?' asked James uneasily.

'Oh, nothing at all—she just came into my mind when I was thinking about the derivation of "gloaming".'

James poured out the coffee.

'Darling, I don't want to go *on* about it, but I do hope you weren't *too* unkind to poor Miss Sharpe.'

'Of course I wasn't,' said James indignantly. 'Miss Sharpe' didn't sound like Phoebe, anyway.

'Don't get cross with me—but she did look rather the kind of girl who might not find it very easy to attract a man.'

'She's not elegant or glamorous, certainly. It was just . . . Oh, why do we have to talk about her? I'm not going to see her again.'

'You are not going to see her again,' Leonora repeated slowly, not so much asking a question as stating a fact.

'No. I had this letter from her thanking me for those cigarettes, and she said she was leaving the cottage and going to Majorca for the winter on the money she's earned—to write a novel or something.'

Leonora smiled in the half darkness. This was most satisfactory news. 'One doesn't like to see people hurt,' she said gently.

'Oh, Phoebe will be all right—please don't let's talk about her anymore.'

'We won't, then. I only wanted you to know that I do understand about everything. And you mustn't think that I'd stand in your way if ever at any time . . . Some beautiful cultured girl, about twenty-two or three,' Leonora mused. 'Darling, I should positively *throw* you together. Interested in the arts and antiques, of course . . .' Here she stopped, for it had suddenly occurred to her that such a girl might very well be working in Christie's or Sotheby's at that very moment.

'Would you like some crême de menthe with your coffee?' asked James, eager for a change of subject.

'*Crême de menthe*,' Leonora echoed with exaggerated emphasis, 'of *all* things.'

'I thought it was your favourite liqueur.'

'Darling, it was and is. I was just thinking of the last time I drank it.'

'When was that?' asked James suspiciously.

'One evening when Humphrey dropped in and the rain came through Miss Foxe's ceiling—*your* ceiling, now—what ages ago it all seems.' How Humphrey had *loomed* over her. Looming in the gloaming—she couldn't really share the joke with James.

'Well, nothing like that's going to happen this evening,' said James.

'No? But of course not.' Again Leonora smiled in the darkness. Would she have minded if it had been *James*? she asked herself, not for the first time. 'Come and sit by me,' she said.

'I'll sit here on the floor,' said James, getting a cushion.

'Then I shall stroke your hair. How curly it is! Like golden wires or whatever the Elizabethan poets said.'

No English literature, please, said James to himself; for having disposed of Phoebe, he did not at this moment want to be reminded of Ned.

XVIII

The next day was Saturday, but the promised visit from Ned did not materialise. He would hardly bother to come all this way, James decided, and certainly not without telephoning first. Once the phone did ring, but it was a wrong number. When evening came James tried to settle down with a book, but he couldn't concentrate; there was a prickly feeling in the back of his throat and he began to wonder if he was getting a cold.

On Sunday morning he woke to the sound of a church bell ringing for the eight o'clock service. It was the church Miss Foxe used to go to, Leonora had told him. He could see its spire without getting out of bed. He turned over again and slept heavily, with vivid dreams of himself and Ned in Portugal, until half-past nine. He realised now that he *had* got a cold and lay pitying himself and wishing that somebody would bring him a cup of tea. But Leonora would not disturb him, he knew, and if he wanted tea he must get out of bed and make it himself. He lay for a while longer looking round the room, admiring the way Leonora had arranged his furniture and objects, better than he could have done himself. The only thing missing was the fruitwood mirror. Had he lent it to Phoebe and had she kept it? He puzzled over this but could not remember and in his weak state it seemed not to matter. When he sat up his head swam and he felt dizzy; perhaps it was something worse than a cold. He was sure he had a temperature.

Leonora, preparing her Sunday lunch, was conscious of the silence up above as she was of any sound, or lack of it, that came from the flat. No doubt James was having a nice long lie-in, she thought indulgently. He was still young enough to be able to sleep late in the mornings, which she never could now. How delightful it would have been to take breakfast up to him — she imagined the artistically laid tray — and to discuss the Sunday papers. But she mustn't bother him or he might fly away. All she had done was to creep up very quietly at about half-past eight to lay his papers outside his door. Perhaps he would call on her later in the day for a drink or a little supper. In the meantime — well, one had one's own Sunday routine which, for Leonora, included a little sleep in the afternoon with the papers or a book. One really needed it at one's age if one was to appear fresh in the evening.

Just after four o'clock she woke up and put on the kettle for tea. There was still no sound from James's flat; perhaps he had crept quietly out of the house while she was dozing. How odd it was, she thought, the way each of them crept about, so very careful not to intrude on or disturb the other. Surely this was the secret of their perfect relationship?

She was drinking her tea when the front door bell rang. Humphrey, perhaps, or her friend Liz? Whoever it was, she took out her powder compact and applied fresh lipstick before going to the door.

A stranger stood on the doorstep, a fair-haired young man – perhaps not all that young, she decided on a second glance, but younger than she was and certainly most attractive and personable.

'You must be Miss Eyre,' he said, 'Leonora – that's how I always think of you, I'm afraid – you don't mind, do you? Jimmie's told me so much about you.'

Leonora was instantly on her guard, she could not have said exactly why – perhaps hearing James called 'Jimmie', though it was more likely that the young man's appearance and air told her that this friend of James's was not quite like Jeremy or Simon, his old schoolfellows.

'I'm sorry, he isn't in,' she heard herself saying, and this wasn't exactly a lie because now that she came to think of it she was certain she *had* heard him go out while she was resting.

'Oh, that's a pity – I suppose I should have called him first to make sure. I did say I'd be in London this weekend. Never mind.' Ned made as if to go. 'Perhaps you'd just tell him it was Ned.'

'Ah, then you must be the American James met on his travels.'

'The same.'

'Won't you come in and have a cup of tea?' Leonora asked. She had the feeling that Ned mustn't be allowed to slip away and that she must take this opportunity – perhaps the only one she would ever have – of finding out more about him.

'Thank you – that would be nice.' Ned stepped into

143

the hall, his glance moving towards his reflection in the fruitwood mirror and resting there for a moment.

The antagonism between them was of the coolest and most polite, almost like the feeling between herself and the woman in the shop where she had bought James's birthday present, but here there could be no happy compromise. It was to be a confrontation in daylight and at the tea table, Leonora realised, dealing as calmly as she could with the business of getting an extra cup and saucer and pouring tea. The word that had suggested itself to her—'confrontation'—was not one she would normally have used, but it seemed peculiarly appropriate as she listened to the quiet American voice, polite and charming, making the most agreeable small talk.

'How my mother would adore this room,' he said, gazing around him. 'She just *loves* everything English. What pretty china you have — and this is Earl Grey tea, isn't it?'

Talk of mothers and tea was reassuring but Leonora's feeling of uneasiness persisted. She knew instinctively that Ned was far more of a danger than Phoebe could ever have been. This was something she had always been afraid of in her relationship with James, and it seemed 'unfair' that she should have to face it on a Sunday afternoon, when few women past their youth feel at their best.

And now Ned was looking at her in a most curious way. His eyes moved from her face, down over her body and legs; even her feet did not escape his scrutiny. She was reminded of the way a certain type of man, particularly, perhaps, a 'foreigner', would 'undress you with his eyes', as the old-fashioned saying put it, except that Ned's appraisal was completely lacking in sexuality or desire. But after a while Leonora realised what he was doing—simply calculating the cost of her clothes and everything about her, including her hairstyle, make-up, jewellery, and even her shoes.

He must have been aware that she knew this for he smiled and, leaning forward, touched the sleeve of her blouse with the tip of one finger.

'Wild silk?' he enquired, the soft questioning note in his voice giving the words a sinister implication.

'Yes, it is,' said Leonora, drawing away from him.

'Jimmie always said you had beautiful clothes and I can see that he was right.'

The words were flattering and Leonora loved compliments; but however charming he might appear this young man wanted to take James away from her and she was not going to let him.

'How convenient that you had this apartment for Jimmie to move into,' Ned went on smoothly. 'It'll be so handy for him. He told me all about your charming house.'

Leonora did not like to think of the two young men discussing her, as she supposed they must have done. She would never know if James had been loyal to her.

'You've come to do some research in the British Museum, I believe?' she asked.

'Oh, my wretched thesis!' Ned was a charming *enfant terrible* for the moment. 'I wonder if I'll *ever* get it done.'

'What's the subject?'

'A study of some of Keats's minor poems.'

'Ah, Keats,' said Leonora, feeling on safer ground. But Keats was not a favourite poet of hers and she couldn't for the moment recall any of the minor poems.

Ned had picked up from the mantelpiece an alabaster dove, a present James had once given her, and was stroking it. She noticed what small hands he had.

'I guess you must know his poem about the dove,' he said.

'The dove, of course.' But again the poem eluded her. Ned began to quote,

> 'I had a dove and the sweet dove died;
> And I have thought it died of grieving . . .'

'Ah, yes, of course, that sad little poem.' Leonora was relieved that it was something so simple and harmless. Whatever had she expected? 'It died,' she said rather foolishly. 'Would you like some more tea?'

Ned passed his cup and went on with the verse, his voice lingering over the words and giving them a curious emphasis.

> 'O, what could it *grieve* for? Its feet were *tied*
> With a single thread of my *own hand's* weaving.'

'You must go and see Keats's house in Hampstead,' Leonora said, agitation rising in her, for now the harmless little poem seemed almost to have some obscure and unpleasant meaning. But that was fanciful and ridiculous, surely. 'We might all go together,' she said more firmly. 'I don't think James has ever been.'

'I'll look forward to that,' said Ned, getting up. 'And now I must go. It's been wonderful meeting you. You'll tell Jimmie I came?' There was a note of teasing doubt in the request.

'Yes, I'll tell him, of course — and you must come to luncheon.'

'*Luncheon,*' he savoured the word as something

peculiarly English, 'that'll be delightful.' He crinkled up his eyes in a smile and was gone.

Leonora closed the front door and leaned against it. She found that she was trembling. She had stood up bravely to her ordeal, she felt, and it had certainly been a good move to suggest some future meeting, but the poem lingered in her mind. Would other people — would James himself — see their relationship like that? she wondered. Going to the fruitwood mirror for reassurance she saw that she looked pale and tense. She felt suddenly too old to fight, but was one ever too old to fight for one's love — would one's hold on that be as tenacious as on life itself? She had always seen herself as a weak woman relying on men — especially on men like Humphrey — to help her through the daily round, but when it came to a real crisis perhaps she was stronger than any of them. Certainly stronger than James.

James had slept through most of the afternoon and woke up when it was beginning to get dark. At one point he thought he had heard the front door bell ring and Ned's voice, but when he tried to listen there was silence and he decided he must have been dreaming.

Now he got out of bed and put on his dressing-gown. He felt lightheaded and in need of something to eat and drink, he couldn't decide quite what. He went to the door and opened it, thinking he would go down to Leonora's flat, but the house was silent. Perhaps she had gone out.

'Leonora!' he called.

'Why, James, I thought you'd gone out. Have you been here all the time?'

'Yes. I woke up not feeling well and I've been sleeping most of the day. I've got flu or something.'

'My *poor* James—I had no idea. Have you had anything to eat?'

'No, I didn't feel like it and I hadn't the energy . . .'

'Get back into bed and I'll bring you something.'

When Leonora returned with the artistically laid tray—soup and toast, scrambled egg and a bunch of black grapes—James had arranged himself on his pillows and was already feeling better. It was that time on Sunday evening when the bells start ringing for Evensong, which can be pleasant or melancholy according to one's circumstances.

'How soon it gets dark now,' said Leonora, going to the window, 'and all the sycamore leaves are falling —the garden's full of them.'

'I'll tidy them up when I'm better,' said James. He hated gardening but perhaps it was the least he could do for her.

They stayed in contented silence for a while, James picking delicately at his food and Leonora sitting on a chair by his bed.

'Oh, by the way,' she said at last, 'I had a visitor this afternoon.'

A visitor—so he hadn't been dreaming.

'Your American friend, Ned.'

'Ned? What's *he* doing in London?'

'Working at the British Museum, I gathered—he said he'd told you.'

James felt himself flushing at the cool tone of her voice, so lacking in reproach. It would have been better if she'd made a scene. He couldn't remember now what

he had told her about Ned. Certainly not· a great
deal. Really it could be said that he had deceived her
again—first Phoebe and now Ned. He turned away
towards the window. He could see a few leaves drifting
down from the sycamore tree. Ned called this time of
year the fall. He had a sudden impulse to run down and
bury himself in those leaves, covering over his head and
body in an extravagant gesture of concealment, return
to the womb or whatever one called it. But then he
imagined Leonora's cool laughter or her unspoken
'understanding'. He would never find a flat of his own.
There was no escape from anything, ever. Now she was
urging him to eat a few grapes.

'One should always have grapes in the house,' she
said, 'one never knows when they'll come in useful.'

'What did Ned say?' he asked.

'Oh, he was very charming. I'm thinking of giving a
little luncheon party and asking him to meet a few of
our friends. He's really sweet.'

Hardly *sweet*, James thought, and yet now that
Leonora had taken him over, who knew what he might
become? She would arrange or adapt him to her
satisfaction just as she had arranged Phoebe. Not to
speak of the way she had arranged James himself. Yet he
had the feeling that Ned might not be so easy to deal
with. There was something basically intractable about
him that would resist any kind of 'arrangement' on
Leonora's part . . .

'You and me,' Leonora was saying, 'and Humphrey
and Liz, of course. Do you think we need ask another
woman? Whom do you suggest?'

'Miss Caton,' said James flippantly.

'Darling, you are naughty! What a pity poor Miss Sharpe has fled to Majorca. I should have liked an opportunity to get to know her better, and Ned would have adored her — all that English literature.'

James reached out his hand and took another grape. He wished Leonora wouldn't go on like this, for after all he wasn't quite himself. He closed his eyes and to his relief she stopped talking.

XIX

There was no doubt in Leonora's mind that something must be done about Ned, but ruthless action, even if it lay within her power, was apt to be upsetting and exhausting. It might well turn out to be like Hercules cutting off the Hydra's head only to find that another had sprung up in its place. Obviously Ned was not to be as easily got rid of as Miss Foxe or Phoebe, who had so conveniently removed herself, yet he would be in England only for a year, such a short time compared with the whole of life. Starting with the lunch party today and then the visit they had planned to Keats's house, what fun the three of them—Leonora, Ned and James—might have together. An exciting and dangerous prospect opened before her as she thought of it. Perhaps it would be best to reach a compromise whereby Ned could be woven into the fabric of their lives in such a way that he became an unobtrusive thread in the harmonious tapestry of the whole. Yet when he came into the room he immediately took the centre of the stage, the glitter of his personality making Leonora seem no more than an ageing overdressed woman, Liz a shrewish little nonentity, and James and Humphrey a callow young man with his pompous uncle.

'Leonora, how *wonderful* to see you!' Ned's lips brushed her cheek, while his soft little hand rested for a moment on her arm.

She had not expected him to kiss her after only one meeting and it occurred to her that when it came to weaving people into the fabric of one's life he had perhaps stolen a march on her.

James, handing drinks like a silently efficient manservant or hired waiter, was dismayed and embarrassed at the way things were going. He wished now that he had never mentioned Ned in that letter to his uncle, for it had not occurred to him that Humphrey would tell Leonora, that Ned would call at her house or that the two of them would get together in this unexpected way. He should have kept it all a secret — as he had kept Phoebe secret — but how could he have foreseen the way things would develop between him and Ned? Surely Leonora was not going everywhere with them? He brooded sulkily over this prospect and went with a bad grace into the kitchen to bring in the joint, a splendid piece of beef.

Humphrey rose to carve it. He was one of those men who are at their best with a carving knife and here was meat worthy of his talent.

'A terribly *English* meal, I'm afraid . . .' Leonora turned apologetically towards Ned.

'Roast beef — that's great!' Ned smiled charmingly back at her. 'And Yorkshire pudding, too — you must have known it was my favourite thing.'

Leonora was gratified to see what good appetites the men had, but she was too emotionally exhausted to eat much herself. Being with Ned was a great strain and James had hardly spoken a word since he arrived — what could be the matter with him? When Humphrey and James went away to the shop, taking Ned with them, she hoped Liz would leave too. But Liz, in the manner of some women, was determined to get the washing-up done and made for the kitchen where she proceeded to scrape up any bits of meat that were left into a dish for her cats.

'James seems very taken with his new friend,' she observed.

'Oh? I didn't really notice,' said Leonora casually.

'I was watching him when you were talking to Ned—his face was a study, as they say.'

'Yes, poor James, he did get left out of the conversation, somehow. It's so difficult, isn't it, to bring everybody in.'

'I wouldn't trust Ned any further than I could throw him,' said Liz rather smugly.

'Well, it's hardly a question of trusting him, is it?'

'Oh, no—we're well out of it, my dear.' Liz spoke with the detachment of one who is past all emotional involvements, and by including Leonora with herself she was perhaps trying to warn her to draw back while there was still time. Yet another part of her wanted her to go on, to find out whether it was possible for the cold, proud and well-organised Leonora to suffer as she had suffered and so to provide an interesting spectacle, a kind of diversion from the boredom of everyday life. 'I wonder what Humphrey thinks about it,' she added, seeing that Leonora did not answer.

'It's not at all convenient,' said Humphrey irritably. 'You know I don't like leaving Miss Caton by herself in the afternoons.'

It sounded almost as if his uncle feared she might be attacked or raped by a prospective buyer, thought James. 'She can cope as well as I can,' he said. 'And I did promise Leonora I'd take her and Ned to see Keats's house. He has to go there for his work, you know.'

Humphrey was silent, confronted by the force of a promise to Leonora and Ned's 'work', though the latter cut no ice with him, as he put it. He was at a loss to understand this new turn things had taken since Ned had come into their lives. What was James up to? First a mistress and now a lover. And why was Leonora making such a fuss of Ned? For all his charm it was obvious that she didn't like him. How much more sensible it would be for her to admit defeat and give up.

'Very well, then,' he said at last. 'I shouldn't like you to disappoint Leonora, of course, but don't make·a habit of it. A pity it's such a wet afternoon,' he added, not without satisfaction.

Leonora came out to the car in the beautiful iridescent raincoat she had worn when she went to meet James at the air terminal. One was not at one's best in the rain, obviously, and one needed to be that now as never before. She had pictured a golden autumn afternoon for the excursion — season of mists and mellow fruitfulness, wasn't it? — and in the past she and James had always been lucky in their weather.

'I seem to have brought rain,' said Ned complacently, as he kissed her cheek. 'It was really glorious *yesterday*.' He glanced at James, half smiling, but James was helping Leonora into the car and it was she who intercepted the look.

Yesterday had been Sunday and a fine day, certainly; she had heard James go out soon after breakfast and not return till late in the evening. She had tried not to imagine where he might have been and had made a point of not asking.

'We shan't be walking about outside,' said James, 'so there's no need for any of us to get wet.'

All the same, the overcast skies and dripping rain spread a pall of sadness over the little house, with its simple bare rooms. There was nobody else looking over it except for a middle-aged woman wearing a mackintosh pixie hood and transparent rainboots over her shoes. She was carrying a shopping bag full of books, on top of which lay the brightly coloured packet of a frozen 'dinner for one'. Leonora could see the artistically delineated slices of beef with dark brown gravy, a little round Yorkshire pudding, two mounds of mashed potato and brilliantly green peas. Her first feeling was her usual one of contempt for anybody who could live in this way, then, perhaps because growing unhappiness had made her more sensitive, she saw the woman going home to a cosy solitude, her dinner heated up in twenty-five minutes with no bother of preparation, books to read while she ate it, and the memory of a visit to Keats's house to cherish. And now she caught a glimpse of her face, plain but radiant, as she looked up from one of the glass cases that held the touching relics. There were tears on her cheeks.

Leonora moved over towards a small conservatory where some late flowers, begonias and pelargoniums, were still in bloom. Bunches of grapes hanging from a vine reminded her of Phoebe's cottage. How simple that had been compared with this! Depression overwhelmed her and seeing James and Ned some distance away, talking together in low voices, she felt as if she were already defeated. She wished now that she hadn't come. Keats meant nothing to her except Ned's voice on that Sunday afternoon, quoting those horrible lines about the dove.

'Fanny Brawne's *engagement* ring!' he exclaimed in his rapturous way. 'And the stone is almandine, it says here. What *is* it, Jimmie?'

'I've no idea,' said James, to whom Keats also meant nothing.

'It looks like a garnet,' said Leonora, who had now joined them.

'Yes, I do believe it is,' Ned agreed. He put his hand on her arm and gazed intently at her. 'Leonora, I think you want your tea. You look *exhausted*,' he added gently.

'Have you had enough, Leonora, *are* you tired?' James sounded as solicitous as ever, but now she wondered if he would have noticed if Ned had not spoken first.

'Of course I'm not tired,' she said rather sharply.

'It *is* tiring wandering around museums—I know Mother always finds it so,' said Ned, 'and I do feel a bit guilty. But if you could know what this *means* to me . . .'

Leonora found herself wondering if it really did mean all that much to him. 'Of course I understand,' she said, 'and it was my idea to come here, anyway.'

But now Ned, capricious as a child, suddenly decided that he had had enough. He demanded tea, and they must have muffins or hot buttered toast. And after that they must go and see the flat he had found for himself, 'Ned's pad', as he called it.

Curiosity and a certain doggedness which a fragile

156

woman can display even in the most unpromising situation led Leonora, tired as she undoubtedly was, to go with them to the house near Brompton Oratory ('Catholic services are very much *me*,' Ned had remarked) in which he had taken a furnished flat.

They entered the sitting-room which was in darkness. Ned switched on a reading lamp which gave just enough light for Leonora to obtain an impression of walls patterned in deep olive green leaves—almost a Morris paper—and furniture upholstered in black leather. A large black rug of synthetic fur covered half the floor and in one corner was a red divan heaped with cushions, also of a fur-like material. The general impression was disturbing in some undefined way, perhaps because it was so very much not the kind of room Leonora or anyone she knew would have chosen. It reminded her of the dark unsympathetic basement where Colin served out salads.

'It belongs to an actor who's away filming,' said James, as if sensing that some kind of comment was called for.

'Then it's not your taste?' Leonora asked Ned, feeling that it easily might have been.

'Not exactly—but it's amusing, don't you think? And I do feel the bedroom's rather me.' He flung open a door through which could be seen an exceptionally wide bed covered in mauve velvet.

'Is it a comfortable bed?' Leonora asked, foolishly, she realised.

'I guess so,' said Ned, 'though maybe comfort isn't all I go for.'

'That striped paper is pretty,' said Leonora, doing

her best.

They returned to the sitting-room where drinks were offered. There was Scotch or vodka or crème de menthe. Leonora accepted half a glass of plain tonic water, but she could feel a headache coming on and put it down untouched after the first sip. James had Scotch and Ned made himself a crème de menthe on the rocks. There was a great business of crushing the ice in some special way which he and James seemed to find amusing. Leonora was unable to see why and felt increasingly embarrassed at the atmosphere which seemed to be creating itself around the two young men. She was just about to suggest that James might run her home when Ned said in his sweetest tone, 'Leonora's tired and it's been rather selfish of us to make her stay out so long. We've had a lovely afternoon and now I'm going to ring for a taxi to take her home.'

He was at the telephone — an elegant 'antique' instrument — before Leonora could protest that of course James would take her. Nor did James make any attempt to offer. He just sat in one of the black leather chairs brooding over the ice cubes melting in his glass. When the taxi arrived they both went down with her. Both kissed her, goodbyes and thanks were uttered and they went back into the house together.

'Well, Jimmie, congratulations!' Ned turned towards James and they faced each other in the narrow box of the lift. 'So you finally did it!'

'Did what?'

'Shook off Leonora, of course! I thought she'd *never* go.'

'I felt rather bad about not taking her home,' James

admitted.

'For God's *sake* — we got her a taxi, didn't we? She could've gone home on a bus — lots of people do.'

'Not Leonora, somehow. Perhaps I should give her a ring later on to see that she got home all right.'

'Jimmie, *really*! What are we going to do about this terrible conscience of yours?'

James smiled, more relaxed now that he and Ned were alone together. 'I haven't got all that much of one, really,' he said, 'but Leonora's fond of me.'

'So am I fond of you. We can't go on like *this*. The first thing you must do is to get out of her house.'

'I know. I've been looking for another flat. It was only temporary, my staying with Leonora.'

'Does *she* know that?'

'Yes, of course.'

Ned smiled. After a while he said, 'Well, that's something. When you move away it'll be much easier to drop her.'

James looked startled.

'You just don't bother to call her,' Ned went on. 'She'll soon get the message.'

James made a movement of protest but no words came.

'Will *she* call *you*?'

'I don't know, probably not. She's always been very good . . .' He hesitated, for it seemed wrong to be discussing Leonora like this.

'I can imagine that. She's the proud type who prefers to suffer in silence. Like a wounded animal crawling away to die.' Ned laughed in a light cruel way. 'Jimmie, don't look like *that* — what've I said?'

Ned's words had taken James back to his childhood. They had had a much-loved cat who had been run over. He and his mother had found her in a wood where she had crawled after the car had hit her, dried blood on her mouth, her beautiful fur all dull.

'You don't understand,' he said.

'Believe me, Jimmie, I *do*.' Ned was suddenly gentle, there were even tears in his eyes. It would have taken the most cynically dispassionate observer to discern any hint of complacency in his tone when he added, 'Life is cruel and we do *terrible things* to each other.'

'Yes, that's the worst of it.'

'It's something you just have to accept—I've hurt people too and I've suffered terribly because of it, lain awake nights—oh, all that.'

'Perhaps Leonora will understand,' James began, but Ned was bored with the subject now.

'Gee, I'm *hungry*,' he said, standing up and pacing about the room. 'Let's go out and eat.'

Leonora went to bed at eleven, determined to be 'sensible'. She read for a little while then dropped off to sleep, the book—a large volume of Victorian memoirs—falling heavily to the floor. After some time she woke with a start—there had been a noise somewhere. James going up to his flat, surely. Or had a burglar got in and was he even now creeping up the thickly carpeted stairs? She put on her dressing-gown and slippers, opened her door and stood, listening. All was silent with the dead quiet of the middle of the night. Perhaps it *had* been James coming in; she would just tiptoe up and see if there was a light showing from his flat. But when she got there she saw that a parcel and some letters she had put there earlier still lay outside his door.

'James?' she called softly, but she knew that he was not there. It was three o'clock in the morning and he was with Ned. Was that better or worse than if he had been with Phoebe? she asked herself, trying to look at the situation calmly. Of course in those days when he had had his own flat she hadn't known where he was at night. Would it perhaps have been better not to have that knowledge now?

Suddenly a piercing cry rang out. Frightened, she huddled beneath the bedclothes, until she realised that it was only one of Liz's cats. Now she was wide awake for the second time and there seemed nothing for it but to go down and make tea, a drink she did not much like because of the comfort it was said to bring to those whom she normally despised. Yet there was something by no means disagreeable about being in bed with the electric blanket on and the tray of tea on the bedside table. She sat up, with a pleated chiffon bedjacket round her shoulders, and thought she might read a little Browning, 'Two in the Campagna', perhaps. The memory of its remote beauty and pleasing images comforted her, though she lacked the strength to open the book and find the poem. After a while she began to see things more steadily; had there been anyone to hear her she might have said 'I am Leonora Eyre', as she had at Vine Cottage. Things would be 'better' in the morning. She decided to say nothing to James about his not coming in. She had tried to be understanding about Phoebe; she would be even more so about Ned.

XX

James put down the telephone and returned to his study
of Christie's catalogue of porcelain to be auctioned at a
forthcoming sale, but he could not concentrate. He had
just told Leonora a deliberate lie, and it had been so easy.
'Say you'll be out of town for the weekend,' Ned had
suggested, and she had accepted it without question, just
as she had accepted the other half lies he had been
obliged to tell to conceal some of the practical arrangements of his new life with Ned. Of course she knew
what was going on, he could sense that, and she was
being deliberately 'good' and 'understanding' about it
so that sometimes he almost wished she would forget
her dignity for a moment and make a scene.

'Was that Leonora?' Humphrey asked, when James
did not volunteer the information. 'Have you told her
you've found a new flat?'

'She knows I've been looking,' said James, 'but I
thought I'd wait until the lease was signed and all that
before I said anything to her.'

'I'm dining with her this evening. Would you like me
to say a word?'

James hesitated. He would have been glad to accept
his uncle's offer as being the easiest way out, but he

supposed he must face up to Leonora himself. How was he to do it?

'Leave it to me,' said Humphrey. He got up and began humming a popular tune of the moment. He was in good spirits these days for he was of course seeing more of Leonora than usual, and although he was too tactful to say much to her about James and his new attachment it was obvious that she was grateful to him for planning little excursions into the country, visits to historic houses, and peculiarly delicious meals to take her mind off what was happening, 'and in her own house,' Humphrey told himself. For James's frequent absences must be as painful to her as if he had actually brought Ned to the flat. 'Would you believe,' Humphrey went on, 'that it's nearly a year since we met at that book sale. It seems like yesterday.'

To James it seemed a much longer time, for his year had been crowded with events and people, as the year of a man of twenty-five is likely to be in contrast with the year of a man of sixty. Leonora, Phoebe, Ned — such varied experiences — and he had loved them all, still did, in a way. But now, strangely, it was Ned who claimed all his attention in a way that the women never had.

'You said you'd be out of town for the weekend?' Humphrey asked.

'Yes,' said James shortly, for he had not yet prepared the lie for his uncle and had no idea what further explanation he could provide. Luckily none was called for; Humphrey went out, still humming his tune, and James was left alone with Miss Caton.

'The country can be very nice in November,' she remarked, 'and we've had very mild weather lately. But

I should take warm clothes with you, just in case.'

James agreed politely, amused at the idea of needing warm clothes in Ned's fiercely centrally heated flat. He returned to his work and tried to put Leonora out of his mind. He was glad that Humphrey was having dinner with her this evening. It was the thought of her alone and waiting for him that he couldn't bear. He decided to apply Ned's remedy: when you can't bear to think about something, then don't; and after a while it worked.

Humphrey was not arriving till eight o'clock and the food was all ready, but Leonora was not in the mood for Meg who had asked if she could drop in for a chat on her way home from the office. Any kind of dreary influence was to be avoided if one was to look and feel one's best and Meg was going on about her present state of health and the difficulties experienced by women of 'their' age, not the most propitious of subjects. Tentatively at first, then with growing confidence, she described her own case – a sympathetic *woman* doctor had explained so much. Everything, it seemed, tiredness, depression, tears, feeling of inadequacy, regrets for wasted life, could be satisfactorily accounted for.

Leonora listened with mounting indignation. *She* had never been conscious of feeling inadequate, and while she could hardly deny that she too was a woman it was intolerable that she and Meg could have this in common.

'Apparently it's really good to interest yourself in a younger person, a sort of child substitute,' Meg went on, 'everyone *needs* to love. One should just let one's love come flowing out, Dr Hirschler said'—here Meg gesticulated with her arms—'not bottle it up or be ashamed of it.'

'That might be embarrassing at times,' Leonora observed wondering if she had given Meg too much to drink.

'So we must all fulfil ourselves in our own way,' Meg went on, 'and if things seem to go wrong sometimes we mustn't *stop* loving, that's the point as I see it.'

Leonora wondered if she had somehow given Meg the impression that she hadn't been seeing so much of James lately, for now Meg seemed to be almost sympathising with her, as if suggesting that James had been neglecting her in some way. Even now she could not bring herself to admit, least of all to Meg, that there was anything 'wrong' between her and James.

'It was just the same when Colin first met Harold,' said Meg. 'At first it was very hard for me, but now that they're no longer together . . .'

'Really? I didn't know that.' Leonora's tone brightened a shade.

'Oh, yes—I thought I'd told you. It didn't work out as we'd hoped.' She made it sound almost cosy, the three of them and their hopes.

'What happened?'

'The usual thing. Harold met somebody at the surgery—this person brought in a poodle—or was it a pekingese . . .?' Meg frowned, trying to recall what seemed to Leonora a totally irrelevant detail, 'a small dog, I know, some dental trouble . . . anyway Harold and the dog's owner took a liking to each other and now they've set up house together.'

'How convenient,' Leonora murmured.

'Colin was very upset, of course, but he knows he's always got me. I'm the only person who *never* changes,' Meg declared stoutly, and she looked it, Leonora thought, sitting there in that same old sheepskin coat which seemed to be her only winter garment. Some might have seen a touch of pathos, even nobility, in her, but not Leonora.

'I'm sorry, Meg,' she said, 'but I'm going to have to turn you out. Humphrey is dining with me and he's due at eight.'

'You ought to marry Humphrey,' said Meg, doing as she was told. 'I can't think why you've never married, Leonora.'

Leonora smiled enigmatically. Obviously one had had one's chances, Meg must be well aware of that.

She saw her out, then lingered by the fruitwood mirror. It gave back the usual flattering reflection and she knew that at the candlelit dinner table she would be looking at her best in a black lace dress that Humphrey liked. Perhaps she would let him kiss her tonight. She had cooked his favourite dishes: chicken with tarragon and chocolate mousse. It was not until she offered the latter and Humphrey refused it that she remembered that he hated anything chocolate. It was James who loved chocolate mousse.

'A little cheese, my dear, if you have it—that would round off the meal perfectly.'

Of course one had cheese, several different kinds, Leonora thought, as she went to get it. In the larder misery came over her. She leaned against the edge of a shelf, her forehead resting on the tins—prawns and lobster, asparagus tips, white peaches – that she always kept in case James should call unexpectedly for a meal. It was so long since he had done that now. If only, when she went back into the dining-room, James could be sitting there instead of Humphrey!

Humphrey chose this moment, when she stood there with the Stilton in her hands, to inform her that James had found a new flat and would shortly be moving into it.

'Where is it?' she asked, perfectly in control now.

'Fulham, though they call it Chelsea these days. Property values have appreciated considerably in that area during the last few years and I think it should be quite a good investment for him. After all, if – as one supposes he will – James should one day decide to marry and buy a house, he can always sell the remainder of his lease . . .'

She let him drone on, remarking that it would be convenient for the shop. Then she began to make the coffee.

Humphrey watched her with more detachment than usual. She looked tired, he thought, not quite at her best in the black lace dress. Women of Leonora's generation had the idea that black always suited them but often they were mistaken. He would leave soon and let her get a good night's sleep. He refused the brandy she offered and was on his feet taking his leave of her at what seemed to Leonora an unusually early hour. He kissed her lightly on the cheek and patted her on the shoulder, murmuring something that sounded like 'there, there,' as one might to a child or an animal.

She felt now as if she had been cheated of

something, a warmer show of affection, the kiss she had expected and had decided to allow him. They might even have ended up in bed and it could have been cosy and comforting for her.

'I suppose James will be wanting to move his furniture, then,' she said, as they were saying goodnight.

'Well, I suppose so.' Really, that furniture would soon be falling to pieces at this rate, Humphrey thought. First from James's Notting Hill Gate flat, then into store, then out of store to that cottage in the country, then to Leonora's house, and now to Fulham. 'Don't let it upset you,' he added. 'I can arrange everything.'

'One would hardly let the moving of a few pieces of furniture upset one,' said Leonora at her coldest.

'Well, my dear, if you *should* need me for anything . . .,' said Humphrey, a little deflated. Again he patted her shoulder and she went back into the house, feeling that the evening had not been a success.

XXI

'Jimmie, you really have the most beautiful *feet*—did anyone ever tell you?'

James shook his head; nobody had ever paid him that kind of compliment before.

'Do you go about barefoot much? That could be the reason.'

'Well, not in England.'

'But this doesn't *feel* like England, does it . . .?' Ned stretched himself out on the synthetic black fur rug.

'No, it doesn't feel like anywhere,' James agreed.

'And yet it's *everywhere*.' Ned was about to quote Donne until he remembered that James was totally uneducated in English literature and that with him there could be none of the pleasure of flinging quotations back and forth at each other.

'You know,' James said after a while, 'I think I'll *have* to go and see her.'

'Oh, you mean Leonora. But surely she knows? Your uncle will have told her.'

'Yes, he has. But I can't just have the furniture moved out and not say anything to her. After all, I'm still very fond of her and I don't want to hurt her more than I need.'

'Oh, Jimmie, that conscience again! So you're still fond of her – what does "fond" *mean*? So you hurt her – but that's what loving *is*, hurting and being hurt. Believe me, I *know*.'

They had had this conversation before and it had occurred to James more than once to wonder whether Ned had ever been hurt himself or whether he had always been the one to do the hurting.

'I've had to hurt people so many *times*,' Ned went on. 'Oh, Jimmie, it tears one apart!'

'It might tear the other person apart too,' James observed, with a cynicism unusual in him. 'I'll go and see her tomorrow.'

For a moment Ned looked almost anxious but the shadow soon passed from his face. James would be no exception to the rule that nobody tired of Ned before he tired of them.

James felt nervous standing on the doorstep, waiting for Leonora to open the door. He had left his keys at the shop, otherwise he could have slipped up to the flat and taken a drink to give him courage. But it was four o'clock in the afternoon and it might have seemed odd to her if he appeared to have been drinking at that time of day.

'Darling James!' she exclaimed.

'Oh, Leonora . . .' There had been only a split second's hesitation before they embraced and for a moment it seemed as if everything was going to be all right again.

But when they started to talk it was obvious that things were not as they had once been. Conversation was sticky. Leonora asked politely after Ned and was told that he was well; she inquired after the progress of his thesis about which James seemed less sure. Then James supposed that Leonora must know that he had found a new flat, which of course she did. She also guessed that he had come to arrange with her about when his furniture should be moved out.

While all this was going on they hardly looked at each other. James could see that Leonora had just had her hair done and was wearing a dark blue dress that was new to him. A Georgian paste and enamel brooch – his last present to her – was pinned to the collar. Leonora noticed that James's hair needed cutting – or was he wearing it longer now? – and that he had round his neck a silk scarf she had given him in the early days of their friendship. All this had been gathered from the quick, almost suspicious glances they had stolen at each other. They had not looked into each other's eyes to see what lay there. Neither seemed equal to that.

'Humphrey said he would arrange things,' said Leonora, 'on the day, that is.'

'I'm perfectly capable of arranging my own move,' said James, glad to be able to take out his guilt on his uncle.

'I stopped your milk some time ago,' said Leonora, 'but at first, when it kept coming, I didn't know what to do.'

'I'm sorry, I should have let you know or something,' James mumbled. It seemed to him that only a woman could think of a trivial thing like stopping the milk when one was in the middle of an affair.

'Oh, it was all right. Liz can always use plenty of milk for the cats. She paid me for it.'

'You must come and see the new flat soon,' said James.

'Yes, of course,' said Leonora, turning her head away.

There was a rather long silence. James had a terrible fear that she might be going to cry or make some kind of scene.

'Oh, Leonora,' he began, 'it isn't that I don't love you . . .'

Leonora looked up at him, startled. The word 'love' had not been mentioned between them before.

'I shall always love you,' James went on, hardly making things better, for 'always' had such a final sound about it; it might just as well have been 'never'.

'James, dear, you really are rather stupid,' she said in a cool tone. 'You know I've never wanted to stop you from having your own friends – after all, one isn't a monster. You loved Phoebe and now you love Ned. When Ned goes back to America, as he no doubt will in time, you'll love somebody else.'

'But Leonora, I'm *not* like that. If only I could explain . . .' James moved his head from side to side in hopelessness.

'And now, James, I really must turn you out – I'm dining with an old Italian friend tonight and I want to have a little rest first.'

She did not watch him go but waited until she heard the sound of his car driving away before she went upstairs to gather strength and make herself elegant for the Conte, who liked to eat steak and kidney pudding and drink Guinness whenever he was in London. It gave her only the merest vestige of satisfaction to remember the hurt look on James's face, but she was rather pleased with herself for having had the courage to deal with him as she had. To hear the word 'love' actually spoken might well have been too much for somebody like, say, poor Meg.

The day before James's move Leonora took advantage of a long-standing invitation to spend a few days with the Murrays at their country cottage. She had always rather despised them and of course November wasn't the ideal time to leave London, but she knew that they had every modern comfort and Joan had arranged a party on· the Friday evening which might be quite amusing. Humphrey and James would supervise the moving of the furniture on Saturday, and Liz had promised to look in to see that all was well after they had gone.

The journey westwards in a comfortable first-class carriage did something to soothe Leonora's feelings. There were only three other occupants, two substantial-looking men, occupied with taking papers out of their briefcases and putting them back again, and a young woman deeply absorbed in a paperback with a porno-graphic cover. Leonora was the only person to respond to the summons to tea and found herself placed at a small window table already occupied by another person.

She sat with downcast eyes, as some women do when faced with a strange man. Leonora did not trust the kind of man one was apt to meet in trains, though in her younger days she had been bolder. She had a book with her—Tennyson's *In Memoriam* in a rather pleasing leather-bound edition—which she immediately opened and tried to read, but it was difficult to concentrate, what with trying to pour tea against the jolting movement of the train, and the fact that *In Memoriam* was perhaps not the kind of reading one would have chosen for a meal taken under difficult circumstances. She had really intended to read it in bed at the Murrays', preferably in the watches of the night when she lay sleepless.

She succeeded in having first pour from the shared milk jug and negotiated her own little teapot successfully. Then hot buttered toast was brought and there was the question of what to eat with it.

'Will you have some jam?'

The stranger opposite was offering her first choice of the little pots of jam, holding them out on a plate encouragingly. Raising her eyes she saw that he was a very good-looking clergyman.

'I don't know . . .' Leonora was used to men suggesting or choosing food for her in restaurants, but perhaps this was not quite the same.

'Yellow, red, green or purple?'

'Which would *you* recommend?'

'That depends. Perhaps somebody reading Tennyson would prefer purple?' he suggested, with an air of gallantry.

'Yes, purple, I think; red and yellow would be unsympathetic.' She smiled and looked up at him. Clergymen, however handsome, were *safe*, one felt, though this might well be an old-fashioned notion. It would be all right to flirt with him a little, in the way that only middle-aged people did flirt nowadays.

It turned out that he was going to Malvern—his

brother was headmaster of a school there, He implied, without actually saying it, that it was a pity Leonora was not going to Malvern too.

'I shall be getting out at Moreton-in-Marsh where my friends are meeting me,' Leonora explained.

'Alas . . .' He smiled.

'Together?' The restaurant car attendant was hovering over them ready to make out the bill.

'No, *apart*,' said Leonora quickly.

He was too delicate in his behaviour to attempt to pay for her tea; that would have been very brash, Leonora decided. As she swayed back along the corridor—he had earlier entered a second-class carriage—she felt encouraged by the little episode. She was still beautiful, still 'desirable', if that wasn't putting it too strongly. She could make something of the encounter when Joan drove her from the station.

But in the car Joan went on boringly about having to call at a teashop run by some woman who had promised to make vol-au-vents for the party which hadn't been ready when she had called earlier. And Dickie was bringing some caviare and it had to be spread on biscuits. And did Leonora mind, but she hadn't had time to make her bed yet.

Leonora sat rather stiffly in the car, wondering why she had come. It was ominous, the bed not yet being made, as if she wasn't really expected. She needed to be *very* well looked after this weekend.

When they reached the cottage she felt more hopeful. Dickie opened a bottle of champagne to revive her after the journey and the room they had given her was quiet and looked over the garden. While Joan had been out somebody had made the bed and there were flowers in a pink lustre jug on the bedside table. *In Memoriam* seemed perfectly in keeping with the pretty Victorian objects that adorned the mantelpiece and dressing table. While she was changing, Joan came into the room, ostensibly to have her dress zipped up but really to ask Leonora about James.

'My dear, we've heard such things—can they be *true?*'

Luckily the front door bell rang before Leonora could go into the subject of James. She never minded the first plunge into a party and entered the room with her usual confidence. But the Murrays' friends turned out to be exceptionally uninteresting and Leonora realised now that she was too tired to make the effort needed for sparkling conversation, even if she had wanted to. After the party had been going for some time she found herself stranded on a sofa with an unattached woman in a bright blue dress, who had somehow fastened on to her and who kept eyeing her in a critical way.

'I can see *you* come from London,' she said. 'You look so washed out.'

The woman's own toothy ruddy face certainly didn't look *that*; a glance at it convinced Leonora that one would prefer to look 'washed out', whatever that might mean.

'What do you *do?*' asked the woman. 'Didn't Joan tell me you were in the BBC? I wish they wouldn't play all that dreadful pop.'

Leonora informed her coldly that she was not in the BBC, and that she didn't have a job.

'You mean you do *nothing?*'

'One lives one's own life.'

'But you could do voluntary work, surely?'

The question was not worth answering, but Leonora's silence gave the woman the chance to enumerate all the things she might do—hospital work, old people, mentally handicapped children, the lonely ones, there were so many lonely ones . . .

'Now then, Ba,' said Dickie coming to the rescue, 'everyone's going. If you're quick the Fosdykes will give you a lift.'

'Goodness, is that the time?' The woman, now identified as 'Ba', got up and almost scuttled into the hall.

Suddenly everyone had gone.

'Good old Ba,' said Dickie, 'always the first to arrive and the last to go. Sorry you got stuck with her, Leonora.'

Leonora gave him a faint smile of forgiveness, but there was no forgiveness in her heart. How could he have let it happen?

'Poor old Leonora,' said Dickie when, very much later, he and Joan were washing up the glasses. 'She doesn't seem in quite her usual form.'

'But she's always so elegant and that was a *lovely* dress,' said Joan loyally. 'It was just bad luck she got landed with Ba.'

'She's so cold and inhuman, or something,' said Dickie, 'I always feel I'd like to . . .'

'Now, darling, don't be beastly about Leonora,' said Joan, with a delighted giggle.

'But suppose one *did* . . . That's really just what she needs. Do you think Humphrey ever has?'

'Just *imagine* them—no, I *can't* . . .' Joan was shaking

177

with suppressed laughter now, so that Leonora, lying in bed in the room above, heard what sounded almost like sobs coming from the kitchen. Then of course she realised that it was laughter—Joan and Dickie being silly about something, as they so often were. She wished now that she hadn't come, but it had seemed better to be away when James's things were moved out. But was she going to be able to sleep tonight? The bed, though comfortable, was not her own, and when she looked up there was darkness where the window should have been.

The next day Leonora had one of her migraines. There was nothing she could do but lie in the strange bed, dozing fitfully, being sick, then dozing again, her splitting head full of James's furniture going up and down the stairs, each piece woven into a kind of pattern that was pressing inside her head until she thought it would burst. Every now and then Joan would tiptoe up the stairs, pop her guilt-stricken face round the door and ask if there was anything she wanted. Once she heard Dickie singing, only to be sharply hushed by Joan. She knew that she had cast a blight over the house and that they would never ask her again, but she felt too ill to care.

It was not until the evening that the pain and sickness left her and she sat up tentatively to find that her head no longer ached and that she was able to drink a cup of weak tea. In her relief at being well again, other things seemed better too. Dickie had promised to drive her back to London the next day; she almost looked forward to taking up the threads of her life again.

XXII

Christmas was now almost upon them. It had come round again in its inexorable way, with its attendant embarrassments which this year seemed even more numerous than usual. Ned was going to have to spend it in Oxford with his friends, who were rather hurt by his neglect of them. The evening before he went James took him out to dinner in Chelsea to give him his Christmas present, a pair of expensive cuff links. This had been comparatively easy to choose, for all Ned asked of a present was that it should have cost the giver a lot of money. Leonora's had been much more difficult. The Sunday paper colour supplements offered no advice on what to give an older woman towards whom one was conscious of having behaved badly. Anything like the Victorian 'love tokens' of the past seemed inappropriate, so James eventually chose a picture book of reproductions of Victorian paintings. He knew that Leonora would be disappointed; even if she did not show it in her face, her tone of voice when she thanked him would betray it, as Miss Caton's had when he opened the book of poetry Phoebe had sent him for his birthday. Books as presents were somehow lacking in excitement and romance. He was relieved when he learned that Humphrey was giving her a pair of amethyst earrings and hoped that his uncle's present would in some way make up for his inadequacy, though he really knew it would not. James himself was going to winter sports as usual with what Humphrey called 'a party of young people', making it seem something very remote from himself and Leonora.

'What are you doing on Christmas Day?' he asked. 'We could spend it together if you like.'

'Thank you, Humphrey dear – but I always feel rather guilty about poor Liz on these occasions. It's a kind of *duty* to give her a Christmas dinner. There she is all the time, with only those cats and unhappy memories of that cad of a husband for company, one does rather feel . . .'

Humphrey had always thought Liz seemed perfectly contented in her own way, but he was relieved that he need not entertain Leonora; he liked to spend the day quietly at his club, sleeping and playing bridge.

On Christmas evening Leonora was invited to supper with Meg. There was cold chicken, and Colin, temporarily unattached and on his best behaviour, had made a special salad just like those he served at the snack bar.

'So different from *last* year,' Meg whispered to Leonora when Colin was out of the room. 'That dreadful time . . . I thought he'd never come back, but he did.'

Leonora could have agreed that this Christmas was different for her too, but she had no wish to discuss her situation with Meg. Soon they would be entering into

180

another year, during the course of which Ned would go back to America.

January was bleak and cheerless and the waiting turned out to be less easy than Leonora had expected. Every day that passed brought the time of Ned's departure nearer, but at the same time it seemed to widen the gulf between herself and James. As the month went on it became obvious that James had 'dropped' her completely. Humphrey hardly mentioned him now; it was as if he were dead or had never existed. The days seemed long and hopeless and Leonora began to wish she had not given up working, for a routine job would at least have filled the greater part of the day. Yet she lacked the energy and initiative to find herself an occupation; she remembered the dreadful woman – 'Ba', was it? – she had met at the Murrays' party and the impertinent suggestions she had made about the useful voluntary work one could do. But when Leonora came to consider them each had something wrong with it: how could she do church work when she never went near a church, or work for old people when she found them boring and physically repellent, or with handicapped children when the very thought of them was too upsetting?

Humphrey, sensing that she was in a low state, suggested that she should find another tenant for the flat; obviously James would never come back and it would be less lonely for her to have somebody in the house. It might even be the means of providing her with a new interest. He envisaged a nice woman of about her own age, or a girl student, or even a young couple, but Leonora didn't feel she could endure any of these.

Another woman might encroach on her independence and one never knew what a 'student' would get up to. As for a young couple, they would probably have a baby and she certainly wasn't going to put up with *that*.

Eventually Leonora forgot about the emptiness of the flat and stopped going up there as she sometimes used to just after James had gone. She had always cared as much for inanimate objects as for people and now spent hours looking after her possessions, washing the china and cleaning the silver obsessively and rearranging them in her rooms. The shock of finding that James had taken the fruitwood mirror had upset her quite disproportionately and Humphrey had searched everywhere to find another for her. Sensitive women were really very irritating at times, he had thought; it wasn't even as if the mirror had been a particularly valuable piece. In the end he had managed to get one tolerably like James's, of a pretty design but badly neglected. Leonora had taken a great deal of trouble polishing it and restoring its beauty with loving care. Yet when she looked into it the reflection it gave back was different from James's mirror in which she had appeared ageless and fascinating. Now her reflection displeased her, for her face seemed shrunken and almost old. Or was she really beginning to look like that?

Her love of beautiful objects led her again to make solitary excursions to the sale rooms. She pored over flower books in Sotheby's book room but could not bring herself to bid for anything; she could never hope to be as lucky as that first and only time. Then she would go down to Christie's to see what was on view there. She kept all this secret from Humphrey, choosing times when it was unlikely that she would meet him, for at the back of her mind was the hope that she might run into James unexpectedly. But she never did.

One particularly cold morning at that time of year when it seems that winter will last for ever, she was examining some jewellery at Christie's — fine stones in settings of the Edwardian era and the twenties, the kind of things she and James had so often laughed over, imagining their owners wearing them on unbelievably splendid occasions — when the full realisation of her unhappiness came to her. Her throat ached and tears came into her eyes, not only for herself but also for the owners of the jewellery, ageing now or old, some probably dead. It was all she could do to walk composedly out of the room, down the wide staircase and into the street. She felt lost, uncertain what to do or where to go, and began walking aimlessly. She must have collided with somebody unknowingly, for she was conscious of a woman apologising in a well-bred voice that had a note of surprise in it, as if Leonora were behaving in a peculiar way. One must at all costs avoid making an exhibition of oneself, she thought, pulling herself together and walking on until she found herself outside a café.

It was not until she had been sitting at a table for some minutes that she realised it was a self-service place and also that she had been there with James. Of course he had always fetched the coffee but now she had to go up to the counter and get it herself. This was not at all the kind of thing Leonora liked, though she had not minded going to Colin's snack bar with Meg occasionally, and when she had got her cup and returned to the table she noticed other things to upset her.

The elderly woman clearing away the used crockery seemed even older and more fragile than when she had been here with James. He used to call her 'the Polish Countess', Leonora remembered; she had worn, aristocratic features and muttered to herself disturbingly in a foreign accent. In Leonora's mind there seemed to be a connection between the old woman and the jewellery she had just seen. To make things worse, she now crashed down a heavy tray on Leonora's table on which were piled not only dirty cups, saucers and plates but all kinds of food scraps — sandwich crusts, bits of lettuce and tomato, the remains of cream cakes and even squashed-out cigarette ends — it was really too disgusting.

'Please take that tray away from here,' said Leonora, in an icy voice.

'I must put it somewhere, Madame,' the old woman grumbled.

There was a hostile silence during which Leonora was conscious that she herself belonged here too, with the sad jewellery and the old woman and the air of things that had seen better days. Even the cast-off crusts, the ruined cream cakes and the cigarette ends had their significance. The woman, still muttering, removed the tray and dumped it on another table where a man preparing to tackle a doughnut with a knife and fork — presumably the implements provided — caused Leonora to shudder. She turned her head away and huddled into her fur coat, feeling herself debased, diminished, crushed and trodden into the ground, indeed 'brought to a certain point of dilapidation'. I am utterly alone, she thought.

Fortunately the state of being 'utterly' alone is a rare one. Leonora saw it as applying to herself because James had left her. She would not have counted the friends she still had, like Humphrey and the elderly admirers who took her out to expensive meals, nor yet her women friends and acquaintances. One would almost rather not have had *them* at all. She was therefore dismayed as well as surprised when a woman carrying a cup of coffee sat down at the table and exclaimed, 'Why, it's Leonora!'

Leonora could hardly pretend not to recognise her cousin Daphne, though they seldom met. Quite a smart tweed coat and fur hat, but the sheepskin boots looked clumsy and countrified, was Leonora's automatic reaction.

'How nice to run into you like this,' Daphne went on. 'I'm just up for the day to see the exhibition at the Academy.'

How conscientiously cultured she was, coming up to town for such a purpose, thought Leonora, with something of her usual scorn. All the same, Daphne was a kind woman and perhaps as one grew older there was something to be said for kindness. Leonora found herself not unwilling to accept her invitation to lunch with her at her club.

It was a little unnerving to see quite so many women gathered together in one place. Daphne made no apology —as indeed how could she?—for the absence of men, and there were one or two scattered about in the dining-room, looking remarkably at ease in their surroundings.

'Segregation seems old-fashioned now,' said Daphne in answer to a comment from Leonora, 'and yet one does rather like to have the place to oneself.'

As the meal went on Leonora felt an absurd desire to confide in Daphne. The wine might have loosened her restraint but she was careful to drink sparingly, recognising the warmth she was beginning to feel towards her cousin as a danger signal.

'Have you had flu this winter?' asked Daphne brightly. 'There's been a lot of it about.'

'Yes, I haven't been too well,' said Leonora evasively.

'Perhaps you need something to buck you up,' said Daphne. 'Sanatogen Tonic Wine, I saw an advertisement for it in the underground when I was waiting for a train. It has added iron, you know.'

Leonora glanced at her in surprise, but there was no vestige of mockery in her tone.

'Or Wincarnis,' she went on, 'like one's mother used to take.'

Daphne's mother — Aunt Hilda — certainly not Leonora's mother with the young Italian lover one had been thought too much of a child to know about.

There was a little left in the half bottle of Chablis they had drunk with their chicken. Daphne poured it into Leonora's glass. It looked very pale and weak compared with the imagined richness of the tonic wine.

The waitress brought the menu for them to choose a sweet. As was to be expected Leonora shook her head, almost with distaste. Daphne, who had perhaps hoped for the jam roll they did so well at the club, regretfully also shook her head and murmured, 'We'll just have coffee, thank you.'

'You live alone, don't you?' said Daphne, settling herself down in one of the leather armchairs for an afternoon's cosy chat, Leonora felt. She nodded an answer.

'You don't find it lonely sometimes?'

'No, I never have.'

'Of course you have a lot of friends abroad, haven't you, living there so much. I wonder you don't try to escape the English winter.'

Leonora saw herself 'abroad', sitting at a marble table with a cool drink, watching people through her dark glasses. Or opening the shutters after a siesta and standing on a balcony looking at a distant view of roofs with perhaps a glimpse of the sea in between. Or visiting family friends, old now, who would remember her parents and herself as a girl. She was better off in her own house, rearranging her ornaments and waiting for James.

'I find life in London more amusing,' she said.

'Oh, well . . .' Conversation was obviously beginning to flag. Leonora thanked Daphne for the lunch and even echoed her hope that they might 'do it again sometime'. They parted in the street with no certainty that they would ever meet again.

Leonora, moving away in the direction of Fortnum and Mason, found herself entering that emporium. She wanted to feel soft carpets under her feet and to move among jars of foie gras and bottles of peaches in brandy. A women's club — though it had been kind of Daphne to ask her there — how could people bear such places? One really felt most unlike oneself in surroundings like that.

'Taxi, madam?' The doorman, solicitous as such people always were to Leonora, was holding an umbrella over her, for a few flakes of snow were beginning to fall.

'Thank you, *yes*.' Leonora smiled up at him.

The snow was falling quite thickly now and when she got home the little patio was almost covered. Leonora stepped out to look at it and as she did so, one of Liz's cats came up to her crying and rubbing itself against her legs. How had it got over from next door? she wondered. She tried to send it back over the wall but the animal would not go and continued to weave around her uttering its mournful cries. What did it want? She felt she ought to say something to it, but she could never distinguish Liz's cats by name, and 'Pussy' seemed altogether too feeble and inadequate a form of address. As she puzzled, Liz came to the wall in her usual fussing way, 'Oh, *there* he is,' she said. 'I couldn't think *what* had happened to him.'

One would hardly want to be like the people who fill the emptiness of their lives with an animal, Leonora thought, going back into the house.

XXIII

Ned was bored. It had been amusing to see if he could get James away from Leonora—though the issue had never been in doubt, for when had he ever failed in such an enterprise?—but now that he had succeeded, what was he going to *do* about him? Jimmie was a sweet boy, but as time went on the innocence and naïvety which had first attracted Ned became tedious, even pitiful, and they seemed to have less and less in common. Jimmie was not very intelligent, had little sense of humour and was always 'around' in a way that began to be irritating.

One evening they were at the theatre and in the interval James went to the bar to get drinks. Waiting for him, Ned's glance moved over the crowd, finally lighting on a dark young man standing alone, also waiting to be brought a drink. Their eyes met, they moved towards each other, they made an assignation for the next day, and that was that. It had been a simple romantic encounter just as Ned's meeting with James in the Spanish post office had been. From then on Ned had been forced to practise little deceptions on James—not always answering the telephone, sometimes assuming a foreign accent or disguising his voice in other ways. It was surprising how easily Jimmie could be taken in, but

Ned was coming to the conclusion that maybe he was rather stupid altogether. For instance, dropping Leonora so *completely*—Ned hadn't really meant it to happen like *that*. Women friends must sometimes be gently but firmly pushed out of the way when necessary, but it must be done skilfully.

'My dear Jimmie,' he said, when they were together one evening, 'you don't mean to tell me that you don't call her *ever*?'

'You said it was the best thing,' said James resentfully, 'and the last time we met was so embarrassing, we didn't seem to have anything to say to each other. Of course I've seen her with Humphrey occasionally, but I haven't been in touch with her since Christmas.'

'Not since *Christmas*? Oh, Jimmie, what have you *done*! Leonora was so *devoted* to you, and you talk about *me* being cruel!'

'Well, *she* hasn't tried to get in touch with *me*,' said James, on the defensive, 'and my uncle sees her quite often. He'd tell me if she wasn't well or anything.'

'And then what would you do?'

'I don't know. The situation's unlikely to arise, anyway.'

'I think you should do *something* about it.' Ned's blue eyes were serious and concerned. 'It just isn't *like* you, Jimmie, to be unkind.'

'Well, what do you suggest?'

Ned hesitated, then looked at his watch. 'Jimmie, I can't suggest *anything* right now because I'm expecting this friend of my mother's that I told you about.'

'All right, then, I'll go. Shall we have lunch tomorrow as usual?'

'I'm not *quite* sure about lunch—I'll call you.'

'I suppose you've got to take her to see the Tower of London,' said James, with an attempt at sarcasm.

Ned laughed. 'The Wallace Collection, more likely,' he said. 'My mother's friends are *vurry* cultured ladies.'

As James got out of the lift a dark young man was waiting to get into it. Their fingers touched for a moment as they politely handed each other in and out of the gates.

James got into his car and drove away, feeling obscurely worried. When he got home he poured himself a drink and sat looking around him. The rooms in his new flat were larger than in his old one and displayed his furniture and objects to better advantage, yet he did not really like it. The evening stretched before him and he had nothing arranged, having assumed that he would be spending it with Ned.

'We don't seem to see much of Miss Eyre these days,' said Miss Caton regretfully. 'Now that the weather's so nice, really quite like spring this morning, perhaps she'll pay us a visit.'

'Yes, Miss Caton, she very well may,' said Humphrey smoothly.

James, who was studying a catalogue and marking items to view, said nothing. He had given some thought to what Ned had said about getting in touch with Leonora but found himself incapable of taking any action. One morning not so long ago he had seen her in Bond Street, but luckily—that was how it now seemed—he had been able to turn into a side street before coming face to face with her. He could have sworn that she hadn't seen him but of course he couldn't be absolutely sure and for some hours after the incident he had been haunted by doubt. It wasn't that he didn't *want* to see her, but the idea of such a meeting was somehow shameful as well as embarrassing—he wouldn't have known what to say.

'That little Rockingham basket,' Miss Caton continued, 'I know Miss Eyre would like that. Very much her style, I thought when I saw it. She's always so smart,' she added, 'so beautifully dressed.' Miss Caton had a plain woman's unselfish interest in the clothes of somebody more elegant. She did wonder what Miss Eyre had bought this spring, what her 'colour scheme' would be. 'You'd think she'd be married, somebody like that,' she went on boldly, for she did not usually talk in this way to Humphrey or James and she realised they might think she was taking a liberty in seeming to comment on Leonora.

'Many women remain unmarried,' said Humphrey, 'there's nothing surprising about it. Being unmarried has its own status—why, you yourself,' he added with absent-minded gallantry, and then stopped in dismay at what he had said. But Miss Caton thought too little of herself to rise to the implied compliment and the moment passed off without embarrassment. Humphrey promised that he would bring Leonora to the shop one day to see their new acquisitions and Miss Caton appeared satisfied.

Humphrey and James were going together that afternoon to view the lots James had been marking in the catalogue. James would indicate what he thought might be worth bidding for and how much it would be prudent to go up to, while Humphrey would tell him why he disagreed with him. It was a game they both enjoyed but James seemed listless and preoccupied this afternoon.

'Isn't that where your American friend lives?' Humphrey asked as the dome of Brompton Oratory came into view.

'Yes, we're just passing the block,' said James looking away from it. Lately he had found himself wondering what Ned might be doing at a given time, when before he had always known.

'I suppose he'll be going back to America soon?'

'Yes, I suppose so.'

'Leonora finds him quite delightful—she's often said so.'

'Older women do seem to like Ned.'

'There's nothing so surprising about that. After all, Leonora was—is—very fond of *you*.'

They walked on in silence for a time. Humphrey felt that he ought to say something to James about Leonora but he could not decide what words to use. At the back of his mind he was conscious of a feeling of resentment towards his nephew. When Phoebe had first appeared on the scene Humphrey had hoped that Leonora might turn to him; when Phoebe had been succeeded by Ned he had been certain that she would. But the reverse had happened and now even the pleasant earlier relationship he had enjoyed with Leonora was in danger of being spoilt. Humphrey now felt that he was in some way responsible for James's behaviour and an element of guilt had crept in so that his presents to Leonora were becoming more expensive and the bunches of flowers more lavish, as if to atone for something that wasn't even his fault.

'What happened, exactly?' he said at last. 'What went wrong between you and Leonora?'

James looked at his uncle in surprise. Surely he must know the answer to that question? If he didn't there was no basis for discussion. He shrugged his shoulders as if to dismiss the subject and they went into the sale room.

XXIV

Leonora loved May—it was almost her favourite month, with tulips and irises in her patio and glimpses of lilac and laburnum over distant garden walls. This year she followed her usual custom of buying new clothes and changing her sophisticated winter scent for the lighter fragrance of lily-of-the-valley. Although it seemed as if a part of her had died in the hard cruel winter which had taken James from her, the spring had revived her in some way so that she felt almost as she had when a girl in that generation which had grown up in the late thirties, still expecting and seeking—though rarely finding—the phenomenon of 'romantic love'. In those days she had gone about in eager anticipation of such an experience but when she seemed to be on the threshold of it she had always drawn back; something had invariably been not quite right. Now, of course, one did not expect anything like that, or indeed anything at all, but on a fine evening she would sometimes go into one of the rooms at the top of the house and look out along the road.

One evening she was standing in the room which had the bars on the window—those bars she and James had joked about so light-heartedly when he had first moved in—when she saw a young man walking along towards the house. James had never come to see her on foot and it saddened her to realise that she didn't even know what his new car—bought that spring, as Humphrey had told her—looked like.

Leonora's long sight was excellent and she had recognised the young man long before he reached the house. It was Ned. She was dismayed at the effect that seeing him had on her—everything came back to her in a rush. For a moment she thought of pretending not to be in, but then her natural courage took possession of her. Ned was still an enemy to be fought. She went into her bedroom and did what was necessary to her appearance, then sat down and waited.

Ned had imagined himself walking along this tree-lined road in the early evening sunshine, bringing Leonora what she could only regard as good news. He had wondered what flowers he should take and had in the end decided on a simple tribute of lilies-of-the-valley, seeing the simplicity of the flowers reflected in himself, almost as if he, still a boy in his mother's New England garden, had picked them with his own hands.

'Why, *Ned* . . .' Leonora's surprise sounded almost genuine, but Ned also had excellent long sight and he had seen her in the distance looking out as he approached the house.

'Leonora, my dear . . .' Their cheeks touched briefly and for a moment her lily-of-the-valley mingled with his Mitsouko.

'Obviously these are *your* flowers,' he said, thrusting the bunch towards her with a shy gesture, almost like a child presenting a bouquet to a royal personage. 'But I suppose your garden's full of them—I might have thought of that.'

'Not at all—I haven't got any and I do love them so. They'll go beautifully in this.' Leonora began arranging the flowers in a Victorian glass vase painted with sprays of forget-me-nots.

'I feel somehow that James gave you that,' said Ned gently.

Leonora did not answer, but busied herself with offering and pouring out drinks.

'It's partly about Jimmie that I've come to see you.'

'Oh?' Leonora had not yet asked herself *why* Ned had come; of course it could hardly *not* be connected with James in some way.

'You've changed the arrangement of this room, haven't you, Leonora? I like it. And you're wearing a *very* becoming new gown that I don't think I've seen before.' Ned's eyes lingered, appraising and pricing everything about her as they had on his first visit.

'What were you going to say about James?' Leonora asked when she could bear the scrutiny no longer.

'Oh, Jimmie . . .' Ned seemed vague. 'Perhaps you'll understand when I tell you that I've come to say goodbye.'

'You're going back to America?'

'Yes, my mother hasn't been too well and I really think I ought to be with her.'

Ned sat primly looking down into his glass, clasped firmly in his little hands, waiting for Leonora's reaction. His life in London had lately become so com-plicated—for the encounter with the young man in the theatre bar had been the first of several -- that flight seemed the only possible solution. Various people, of whom James was the most important, would thus be detached at one blow, for none was in a position to follow him or even to question that his mother needed him.

'She's seriously ill, then?' Leonora asked.

Ned's fractional hesitation, no more than the smallest part of a split second, gave her the answer. 'I'm very sorry,' she said formally, 'but I hope your stay in London has been rewarding—I mean, that you've managed to do all your research on . . .' The memory of the afternoon at Keats's house came back to her and she stopped. 'James will miss you,' she said at last.

'Leonora, he *won't*.' Ned bent forward towards her and made as if to take her hands, but she evaded him. 'That's what I wanted to talk to you about. I had simply no idea . . . I was *appalled* to know that he hadn't been seeing you at all.'

Leonora was stunned for a moment. 'But surely you must have known?'

'I swear I *didn't*. I never dreamed Jimmie could be so . . .' Ned seemed at a loss for words and Leonora did not help him. 'But don't you see, *now*, when I'm gone, it can all be the same again. Believe me, Leonora, if I'd ever *dreamed* . . . When Jimmie *told* me, I couldn't sleep nights for thinking what you must have suffered.'

Leonora did not comment.

'I know Jimmie loves this room,' Ned went on, looking around him. 'All your lovely things . . . he's missed you so much and I expect you've missed him too.'

Leonora tried to say something but no words came. It needed all her strength and self-control to hold back her tears.

Ned was watching her with dispassionate interest, wondering if she would let go and preparing to soothe her if she did. Tears, thought by some to be a woman's most powerful weapon, did not of course move him, but he was good at comforting weeping women. There had been quite a number of them in his life, from his mother to older women and young girls who had been foolish enough to expect more than he was prepared to give. He had seen with distaste many a red face working and blotched with tears, rather as Leonora had seen Meg weeping for Colin. Older women especially were most unwise to cry, it was ruination to their appearance.

Yet Leonora appeared to deal with the situation as elegantly as she did everything else. If he had hoped to see her crumble he was disappointed. Could it be that she didn't still care for Jimmie after all?

'My dear, you needn't mind me,' he said almost kindly. 'We may never meet again. I just want to think of you and Jimmie happy together in your *wonderful* friendship.' He felt generous and good as he said this, and now he really did want it. But his glass was empty; he wished Leonora would refill it and thank him for giving James back to her, but she did neither. Her silence was disconcerting. 'You must *forgive* him,' he went on. That was what women should do and even did, in his experience; they overlooked things, they took people back, above all they forgave.

'But James hasn't asked me to forgive him.'

'He hasn't?' Really, Jimmie might have made things

a little easier for him. 'I expect he will, though, and you mustn't be too hard on him. If he came to you on his bended knees, surely you'd forgive him?'

Leonora said nothing.

'You mean he could come to the door and you wouldn't open it – you'd let him go away? Like that scene at the end of *Washington Square*? Leonora, I'm sure you read Henry James, he's so very much *your* kind of novelist.'

'Of course one has read James.' Leonora tucked the embroidered handkerchief she had been clutching into her sleeve and stood up. 'Goodbye, Ned. I hope you'll find your mother much better when you get home.'

'My mother? Oh, thank you, I'm sure I will. And that reminds me, I suppose I'll have to go to Liberty's and get presents for my female relatives. What do you recommend? – lengths of dress material, I suppose, but I've always wanted to buy one of those leather hippopotami for a particularly *unfavourite* aunt . . .' Ned prattled on in his usual style. 'I've had a *wonderful* time in London, and it's been *great*, meeting you, Leonora. I'm sure that in time you and Jimmie . . .' He looked out of the window, as if hoping to see James crawling painfully towards the house on his knees like some primitive Latin American Catholic pilgrim.

In the hall he glanced confidently at the place where James's fruitwood mirror had hung, but the space was empty and he was denied the pleasure of seeing himself. He turned to Leonora and kissed her, then hurried out of the house. A taxi appeared in the road and he got into it.

Leonora watched him go; she supposed she had acquitted herself quite well, perhaps she had even won a kind of victory, but it hardly seemed to matter now.

The evening sun showed up a few specks of dust on her china and glass objects, so she decided to wash them. It would give her something to do and the result would be satisfying. As she picked up a miniature jug decorated with flowers she noticed that a petal from one of the forget-me-nots was chipped off. How had she not seen this before? She could not bear to have anything not quite perfect in the room and she was just putting the jug away in a cupboard when the telephone rang.

It was Meg. She wondered if she could come round and see Leonora; she wanted to ask her something. Something that would be easier to discuss face to face than on the telephone.

One of the things James had taken from Leonora was the pleasure of being alone which she had enjoyed before she met him. Now she almost welcomed Liz's interruptions or Meg's cosy chats about Colin. She was conscious of sounding quite enthusiastic as she told Meg she would be glad to see her.

'You've done something different to the room, haven't you?' said Meg as she came in. 'Put the sofa in a different place, is that it?'

Leonora poured drinks and they sat down. As she took a sip of her gin she realised that she had already drunk a large one with Ned. She had needed it then; now it made her feel light-headed and unreal as if she were moving in a dream.

'And how's James?' asked Meg chattily. 'I was sure you'd be out with him, or he'd be here, when I rang. Is he away? Gone on one of his Continental jaunts to buy things for the shop?'

'James is . . .' Leonora began, but she found herself unable to go on. The tears she had held back from Ned now flowed and her body was racked with sobs in the most embarrassing way. Helpless as she was, she could still feel a sense of shame at what was happening to her. It seemed the final touch of irony that she should break down in front of Meg of all people. Fumbling for her handkerchief, she struggled to control herself, to produce some explanation for this most uncharacteristic behaviour, but Meg forestalled her with soothing words. She came over to the chair where Leonora was sitting and put her arms round her. Leonora, who found the contact distasteful, tried to shake her off but she was powerless and could not move.

'My dear, I knew how it was,' Meg murmured. 'I guessed—about James. You put such a brave face on it at Christmas, but *I* knew. He's gone, hasn't he . . .?'

Leonora did not need to answer.

'*So* like Colin,' Meg went on. 'I've been through it all so many times. But they always come back in the end, you'll see.'

'*No* . . .' Leonora was surprised at her own vehemence. 'It could never be the same again.'

'That's what you think at the time,' said Meg, 'but you'll see — it'll be all right. You mustn't expect things to be perfect, Leonora, they never are.'

Leonora, now recovering her composure, was beginning to be conscious of how ridiculous Meg looked, kneeling there on the floor, even when she was voicing such noble and unselfish sentiments as the need to accept people as they are and to love them whatever they did.

'What a lot of weeping seems to have gone on in this

room,' she said, with something of her usual cool amusement. 'Is it the gin, or what? Let me refill your glass, Meg. I'm sure you need it.'

'Well, just a very small one with plenty of tonic,' said Meg, going back to her chair.

'You came to ask me something,' said Leonora, 'what was it?'

'Oh, yes. You know the flat at the top of your house – I was wondering if you'd got another tenant since . . . it became empty. Because Colin's brother is looking for a place, *such* a nice young man, I'm sure you'd like him and he'd be a *model* tenant.'

'Oh, Meg, I'm afraid it's impossible,' said Leonora in her sweetest tone. 'I really don't think I could cope with a young *man*.'

'It might be an interest for you,' Meg began, 'I mean . . . Oh, Leonora, what is going to happen to James – and to you – haven't you thought?'

'I shall be quite all right, thank you, Meg, and as for James – who knows? He might even get married.'

'You think so? I'm sure Colin would never *marry*,' said Meg, with a faint air of superiority.

XXV

When it came to the point, James and Ned parted
amicably enough after the terrible scene they had had,
saying unforgivable things to each other and throwing
objects, such as the fur cushions and at one point a heavy
Venetian glass paperweight which had narrowly missed
not only Ned, for whom it had been intended, but the
huge mirror which filled one wall. Ned's eyes had
sparkled – obviously he was enjoying the whole thing
enormously. Such a scene was, of course, only one of
many in which he had been a protagonist. James, hurt
by Ned's infidelities and wounded by the things he had
said, had enjoyed it less, especially as it had been his
jealousy and hurt pride that had started it off. Afterwards, when it was all over, Ned seemed to be almost
his old self again, so that James had been made to feel
rather a fool. 'My dear Jimmie, that's *life* – you mustn't
take things so .*hard* . . .' If Ned had stayed, James
thought – but he had to go back to his mother who, if
she wasn't exactly at death's door, really did *need* him,
and nothing would make him change his mind. It had
been amusing choosing the dress lengths for his female
relatives in Liberty's, not to mention the leather
hippopotamus – 'Aunt Hetty will *die* when she opens
the package' – but in the end parting had come with the

inevitability of the last scene of a well-constructed play.

Now James was on his way to see Leonora. It seemed the only thing left to do and he had the feeling that she would be expecting him. One of the last things Ned had done was to urge him to go and see Leonora. 'Jimmie, she *needs* you,' he had said, and James felt that he was probably right, as usual. However badly one had behaved—and James was prepared to admit that he had undoubtedly managed things clumsily and in a way that had hurt her—Leonora would always be there, like some familiar landmark, like one's mother, even.

It seemed not quite in the best of taste to take her a present or a bunch of flowers. James hoped it would be enough to have brought just himself.

'Why, James . . . and what an elegant new car—*white* . . .' Although she had been anticipating this moment Leonora was surprised when she opened the door and saw him standing there.

Should he kiss her? he wondered. They had always kissed in the past but she made no movement towards him, so he followed her into the sitting-room where everything looked different. He made the usual remark about her having rearranged it.

'I suppose Ned's gone now,' she said. 'I expect you miss him.'

How understanding she was; though James found himself thinking, as he so often had before, that it would have been easier if she had been just a little angry. He hadn't really come here to talk about Ned.

'Yes, I did miss him at first,' he said, 'but towards the end things went wrong, somehow. Ned is rather . . .' He had been going to say 'fickle' but the adjective seemed too naïve and old-fashioned.

'Poor James, one had realised that, of course. I mean, how Ned was.'

Leonora was leaning back in the velvet-covered chair, perfectly relaxed. The evening sun showed up the fine lines on her skin and she looked older than James had remembered, yet still beautiful in her way.

'Oh, Leonora, I knew you'd understand. You were always so . . .' James fumbled for the word that would sum up Leonora's behaviour over Phoebe, and of course over the much more serious matter of Ned.

'Poor James.' She sounded genuinely concerned. 'Time is a great healer,' she added, in a slightly mocking tone, 'but you're still *much* too young to know about that.'

'Don't make fun of me.'

'I'm not,' she protested. 'I imagine you and Ned parted on good terms?'

'Yes, in a way. But we had a terrible scene before he went.'

As she listened to James describing that last quarrel Leonora found herself tempted to laugh. It occurred to her now that Ned was in many ways a comic character but the realisation had come too late. And would it have made any difference if she had seen him as such when he first came into their lives?

'But, Leonora, in the end he *wanted* to go back—he just didn't care about me anymore.'

Leonora was less relaxed now, aware that with this confidence she was receiving more from him than she ever had before, but unable to respond in the way that he obviously expected. She and James had both been hurt, but it hardly seemed to make a bond between them—it was more like a barrier or a wedge driving them apart.

'People do change,' she said. 'One sees it all the time.'

'But not *us*, Leonora. I'm sorry if I hurt you. Won't you forgive me?'

'Yes,' she answered. 'Yes, I forgive you,' she repeated, as if she were not quite sure. One did forgive James, of course; one was, or saw oneself as being, that kind of person. Why, then, did one not make some generous gesture, some impulsive movements towards him, so that all could be forgotten in the closeness of an embrace? Evidently James expected it, for he stood up and came towards her, then hesitated when she did not respond.

'Well, then,' he said, 'where do we go from here?'

'I don't know,' said Leonora.

She wondered how many times Meg must have enacted this kind of scene with Colin, always receiving him back so that as time went on it became easier and no explanation was needed. The bottle of Yugoslav Riesling—his favourite wine, always in the fridge—would be broached, and by the time it was finished all would be well again. Meg would in due course, or perhaps immediately, buy another bottle and keep it there, ready for the next time. But there was something humiliating about the idea of wooing James in this way, like an animal being enticed back into its cage. Even if he had had a favourite wine, Leonora did not think she could have brought herself to produce it. Yet the sherry they were drinking now seemed actively hostile in its dryness, inhibiting speech and even feeling.

If she had chosen something with a more festive air, something sweet or sparkling or warm — even a late cup of tea — would it have made any difference?

James stood up, as if to go. He did not know what to do now. Hopefully he glanced over to the table where the little Victorian flower book used to lie, open at a different page every day, but it was not there. Had she put it away when she changed the room?

'Humphrey is taking me out to dinner,' she said. 'Some new place he's discovered.'

Was it worth trying again? James wondered, not knowing how to take his leave. What would Ned have advised? He moved over towards the window and saw his uncle's car draw up in the road. Humphrey got out of it, encumbered by a large bunch, sheaf, perhaps, of peonies. There was something slightly ridiculous about the exuberance of the flowers and the way Humphrey, doggedly clutching them, went round fussily trying each door of the car to make sure it was locked.

'Goodbye, James,' Leonora was saying. 'It was sweet of you to come.'

The sight of Humphrey with the peonies reminded her that he was taking her to the Chelsea Flower Show tomorrow. It was the kind of thing one liked to go to, and the sight of such large and faultless blooms, so exquisite in colour, so absolutely correct in all their finer points, was a comfort and satisfaction to one who loved perfection as she did. Yet, when one came to think of it, the only flowers that were really perfect were those, like the peonies that went so well with one's charming room, that possessed the added grace of having been presented to oneself.